Looking for
for
TRUE

Tricia Springstubb

MARGARET FERGUSON BOOKS

HOLIDAY HOUSE · NEW YORK

Margaret Ferguson Books

HOLIDAY HOUSE is registered in the U.S. Patent and Trademark Office.
Printed and bound in September 2022 at Maple Press, York, PA, USA.
www.holidayhouse.com
First Edition
1 3 5 7 9 10 8 6 4 2

Library of Congress Cataloging-in-Publication Data

Names: Springstubb, Tricia, author.
Title: Looking for True / by Tricia Springstubb.
Description: First edition. | New York City : Holiday House, [2022] | Audience: Ages
9 to 12. | Audience: Grades 7-9. | Summary: "Jude and Gladys join forces to try
and rescue a dog they think has been abandoned"— Provided by publisher.
Identifiers: LCCN 2022001729 | ISBN 9780823450992 (hardcover)
Subjects: CYAC: Dogs—Fiction. | Friendship—Fiction. | LCGFT: Novels.
Classification: LCC PZ7.S76847 Lo 2022 | DDC [Fic]—dc23
LC record available at https://lccn.loc.gov/2022001729

ISBN: 978-0-8234-5099-2 (hardcover)

For our Julian

Looking
for
TRUE

Jude

Usual. That described Jude's day so far.

Or *rotten. Rotten* worked too.

Eight a.m. and his brother was already on their mom's last nerve. She said if Spider didn't settle down, she'd lock him in the basement till he turned white as a grub. Spider slid his little thumb in his mouth and went quiet. But Spider being quiet never lasted long. Just ask Jude, who'd been stuck babysitting him all summer.

Then, Mom's job at Good Samaritan Nursing Home called her for an extra shift she didn't want to do, only she couldn't say no because they were laying off people left and right and her boss was evil with a heart of coal.

Plus, it was hot. *Hot.* Mom was sweating by the time she got her uniform on. Massive purse on her shoulder, ugly work shoes on her feet. That familiar mix of guilt and relief crept over Jude. He wished she didn't have to go to work. He couldn't wait for her to go to work.

"Chores...your butt in gear or...*Jude!* You listening to me?"

"Huh? Yeah, Mom! I'm listening."

She blew a breath, stepped outside, and got whacked by a bunch of pine needles. He'd planted that tree back in first grade. Everybody in the school got a pine tree that year. Eastern white pine. The trees were the size of toothbrushes, and Jude planted his right by the door. Nobody was more surprised than him how fast it grew.

Mom swung her massive purse at it. Whap! Whomp!

This could've been funny, but no way Jude laughed.

Mom got in her car. At least that pile of junk started up on her first try.

Jude exhaled. Staying on his mother's good side was always hard, but this summer? *Hard* was more like *impossible*.

Soon as she drove away, Spider started in. Jude's little brother was four years old. His real name was Silas but guess who called him that? Nobody, that's who. He could climb anything, which was how he got the nickname. But when he started whining, the bug you thought of was a mosquito.

"I'm hot. I'm bored. I'm hot. I'm bored. I'm..."

A *swarm* of mosquitoes.

"Find your shoes," Jude told him. "We'll go to the library."

While he waited, Jude admired his pine tree. The tips of the branches were so green they practically glowed. Like, *We are alive, dude. We are growing right before your eyes.* In spite of how this day was going, Jude had to smile.

Then. Then along came a lady walking an ugly dog. In this small town, if you didn't actually know a person, you recognized them. But Jude didn't remember ever seeing her. Her hair hung down like it was exhausted, and she was pulling on a cigarette. The way she dragged her feet, you'd think she was headed to her best friend's funeral.

The dog's fur was a mess of colors, gray, brown, and black, with a white stripe down the middle of its face. Something funky about its eyes.

Mom always said *It's a dog, it'll bite.* Back in the day, she went to a party where some guy brought his old dog. Mom felt sorry for it, but when she bent to feed it a corn chip, that mutt sank its teeth into her upper lip. You could still see the scar. Mom's smile had a dent in it.

Jude was no fan of dogs. But this one? When it saw him, its eyebrows went up. Jude didn't even know dogs had eyebrows. Next its tail started waving. Its paws did a funny, nervous dance, and all of a sudden, after all that twitching and switching, it sat down still as a stone. Looking right at him.

The lady didn't notice. She kept going till the leash played out and her arm jerked back. She didn't like that. She threw her cigarette on the ground. Screwed up her mouth. She wasn't old, but her voice was. Like if a fossil talked.

"Move it." She tugged the leash. *Nope,* said the dog. She tugged it harder. "I said move your butt, Spooky!"

Jude tried to beam the dog a warning: *She's getting steamed! Better do what she says.* But it just sat there, eyes glued to him, till the lady yanked so hard the dog let out a strangling sound. Choke collar, thought Jude. Now it started barking. Not like any barking he'd ever heard. Not "woof" or "bow wow," but a whole tangle of sounds. Like baby talk, if the baby was part wolf.

"Mute it!" ordered the talking fossil. She swung her arm up over her head. That made an impression. Tail between its legs, Spooky muted it, all right. This time when the boss lady started walking, Spooky trotted along.

Jude kept watching till they were out of sight.

His rotten day felt even rottener.

In the distance a train whistle blew—two long, one short,

another long. Spider busted out the door, shoes on the wrong feet. He was a fool for trains. Lucky for him since, in this town, a train was pretty much always coming.

Jude locked up the house. The pine tree gave him a pat as he went by.

Gladys

Gladys lay in bed contemplating the puzzle that was the English language. For example, why was *tree* such a short word? Mushy words like *passion*, fuzzy words like *knowledge*, rarely used words like *parabola*—they were all much longer than *tree*. *Sun*, she thought. *Moon*. *Joy*. *Fear*. *Word* itself! Could there be some strange, inverse ratio going on, so the more essential the word, the fewer letters it had?

This was the kind of thing Gladys loved to contemplate.

She fluffed her pillow and rolled onto her back, her preferred contemplating posture, as downstairs a baby began to wail. Two seconds later, another one joined in. Babies are empathetic creatures, Gladys's mother said. They don't know where they end and the rest of the world begins, so they feel the pain of others as if it's their own. Mama, who ran an in-home daycare, was an expert on babies and young children.

"Gladys!" she called up the stairs now. "Can you come help?"

With a heavy sigh, Gladys rolled out of bed and pulled on a sundress printed with smiley suns. Though she was eleven, she was so small she wore clothes made for eight-year-olds. Long ago, before Mama and Dada adopted her, Gladys had "failed to thrive." The doctors said she might still catch up. Gladys fervently hoped so.

She was dragging a brush through her recalcitrant hair when something drew her to the window. A woman she'd never seen before was walking her dog. Not walking. She was *shambling*. The barest possible energy that a living creature could expend, that was how she moved.

But the dog. It was adorable! Not that Gladys particularly liked dogs. When you were Gladys-sized, even a nice dog could knock you down with a whack of its tail or paws. And mean dogs? Well, did anyone like mean dogs? Besides, Dada was ultra-allergic to anything furry, and Gladys could never love anything that made her father sneeze and itch.

So why did this dog tug her heart? Medium-sized, shaggy, it had a head shaped like Mama's garden trowel. Except for the milk-white stripe between its eyes, its fur was black with patches of gray and brown, as if it couldn't decide what color to be. Its tail curled like a fishhook. It might have been a rock at the end of the leash, for all the attention that woman paid it. When she stopped to light a cigarette, the dog gazed over its shoulder mournfully, as if it had left something precious behind.

"Gladys!" Her mother's voice rose above the din of baby wails. "I could really use some help here!"

Gladys called, "In a second!"

The dog heard. It lifted its head, its eyes making direct canine-to-human contact with Gladys, who leaned forward, flattening her nose against the screen.

But then the owner gave the leash such a hard yank, Gladys felt it in her own throat. *Ow!* The woman muttered something. Poochie? Did she call the dog *Poochie*? That was almost as bad as *Gladys*. With another cruel, heartless yank on the leash, she shambled onward.

"Gladys!"

"I'm coming!"

Was Gladys talking to her mother? Or to the dog? She didn't know.

She watched till the crooked tail disappeared from view, then ran downstairs.

Where mayhem ruled. Cheerios were everywhere. You'd never guess how many Cheerios were in a single box till a toddler dumped them all out. Lily Harrison was using a naked Barbie doll's feet to dig in the potted rubber plant, and Jackson Lamott was squealing because he'd gotten stuck under the sofa. Gladys pulled him out and dusted him off.

"What would I do without you, sugar?" Mama jiggled Mateo Brown on her hip. He grabbed the tip of her long red braid and sucked on it, but Mama was too harried to notice. "Angela called off."

Gladys couldn't believe it. Except she could, because this was the second time in a week that Mama's so-called assistant had bailed at the last minute. "You should fire her."

As if that would ever happen! Mama—or as everybody else called her, Ms. Suza—was all about helping people. Parents didn't pay her on time, or picked their kids up two hours late, or persuaded her to babysit on weekends even though the daycare was closed, and Mama always cut them slack. Life was hard enough in this town, she said, especially since the auto plant across the river had "unallocated," which was management's cowardly way of saying "fired every last person's butt." Including Dada's.

A saint, everyone said. *That Ms. Suza is a saint.*

Gladys used to love hearing that. She was proud of her mother and longed to be just like her.

Lately, though. Lately, she wasn't so sure. Mama said if you looked for the good in others you'd be sure to find it, but Gladys couldn't help noticing their faults. Angela, for example. She was a selfish excuse-maker who repeatedly took advantage of kindly Mama.

Had Gladys's birth mother been a fault-finder, too? Was that where she got it from?

Questions like this were something else that was happening more often lately. They kept popping into her head. It wasn't as if she wanted them to. It definitely wasn't as if she knew the answers. But Gladys's brain was made for questions. It wouldn't stop asking them, even when she wished it would.

"Angela has enough trouble without losing her income," Mama was saying. "She's already living on the edge."

Gladys sighed. She got the broom and began sweeping up Cheerios as Sophie Myers, a demon in the guise of a four-year-old, studied her.

"You got a pimple on your chin," she informed Gladys.

"And your hair looks like you brushed it with an eggbeater."

"My mother has hair in her armpits." Sophie picked a Cheerio off the floor and ate it. "And other places, too."

"That's enough information, Sophie."

It was going to be another hot day. Gladys herded the sprouts into the backyard, into the shade of the tree, and painted them all with sunblock. They hated this but they let her, holding out their arms like little scarecrows and squeezing their eyes shut while she did their faces. Moments like this, Gladys experienced complicated feelings toward them.

Look how innocent they were. If a person they trusted told them to hold still while toxic slime was poured over their heads, they'd do it. Their helplessness made them lovable but also pitiful.

The shaggy dog trotted across her mind.

Jude

Jude and Spider walked down Front Street. Past Aunt Annie's Attic, the barber shop, twelve million FOR RENT signs. Like usual, Spider had to stop and look in the window of the old toy store, even though it was nothing but a fly graveyard now.

Just past Freddy's Bar and Grill, a greasy restaurant near the tracks, they stopped to wait for the train. On the other side—the grain mill, the scrapyard, the shut-down canning factory. Empty fields, patches of woods, houses here and there. Till you hit Route 7, basically no-man's land.

Jude and his best friend, Jabari, had their amazing, world-class secret fortress there.

Warning lights flashed and the barriers went down. As the train got near, Jude grabbed hold of his brother's basketball jersey. Train-crazy Spider said the name of every car as it went by.

Every single one was a tank car.

"Tank car tankcar tankcartankcar..."

Next, the library. Jude and Spider loved the place. The librarians were always nice, even to Spider. Their eyes might be saying, *Lord please, not this kid again,* but their mouths would still smile. The library gave out free lunch, plus afternoon snacks. Mom didn't like Jude using her laptop for games, so he played on the library computers any chance he got. Today's bonus: three new train books for his little brother.

When it was time to go, Spider did the Mosquito. He was tired, his legs hurt, he was thirsty, he was *waa waa waa.*

Jude could put Spider on his shoulders and ride him home, but why should he?

"You're not a baby, Spy. You can walk."

"I'm too tired!"

"If I bust your butt you'll really be tired."

Like that would work. Spider knew Jude would never hit him.

Spider was puny, the opposite of Jude, who'd always been bigger than most kids his age. Getting left behind in first grade made him stick out even more. People would ask him, *You sure you're only eleven?* Like maybe he was so dumb he got his own age wrong? Like maybe Jude didn't know when his own birthday was?

Spider lay flat on the sidewalk, doing his roadkill imitation. Some teenagers walked around him, laughing. Jude was ready to yank his little brother upright when, who knows why, he remembered the fossil lady. How she yanked her dog. How Spooky kept barking anyway. That ugly bark made you want to cover your ears, but still. Jude wondered if the dog had always been loco and that's why the lady didn't love it, or if she didn't love it and so it went loco.

He crouched next to his brother.

"Get up before I pop you one," he said.

Guess who said "*Pleeeeeeease carry me*"?

Guess who caved?

Walking along, Spider on his shoulders, Jude named the trees they passed.

"Silver maple. Sweet gum. That one with the sketchy bark? Sycamore."

He'd been hooked on trees ever since he planted that pine. Show him a leaf or a piece of bark, he could name the tree.

When Spider's father, Holden, was still in the picture, he gave Jude a pocket-sized tree identification book. Holden had been gone over a year now, but Jude still had the book. In fact, he had it right now.

"Hemlock. Oak." Hanging on to his brother with one hand, he wriggled the book out of his pocket with the other. Thumbed the pages. "Red oak, to be exact."

Trees calmed him down. Smoothed him out. When the school counselor told him to close his eyes and picture someplace peaceful, Jude imagined a forest. Sometimes he was walking among the trees. Sometimes he was resting his back against one, sunlight sifting down like sugar.

When they got home, Mom was already there, standing in the driveway talking to their neighbor, Mr. Peters. She was holding hedge clippers. Mom was no fan of yard work, so this was a surprise.

"I come home tired as a dog," she was telling Mr. Peters. "I drag myself into bed. The second I lie down, your freaking security light comes on. It shines straight in my bedroom window, right into my eyes." She swung the hedge clippers like they were nail scissors. Her work made her tired but also superstrong.

Mr. Peters took a careful step back. The man had the world's saddest comb-over, and who knew where his chin was. Mr. Peters was retired but still dressed like he was going to a desk job—button-down shirt, pants with a crease. He was all about yard work. Mom said he had a stick up his you-know-what. But he was always nice to Jude.

"The skunks activate it." Mr. Peters looked like such a weakling, his voice was always a shocker. It was deep as the Grand Canyon. "The skunks come out at night and dig for grubs. They ruin my lawn."

"I don't care if it's freaking grizzly bears. This is the second time I'm asking you." Mom still wore her work uniform. It had a streak of something dark and shiny down one side. "I'm trying to be nice. But—"

"Auntie!"

Spider slid off Jude's shoulders as a sleek red car pulled into the driveway. Auntie Jewel climbed out. She looked just like Mom, if Mom went to the hairdresser and got a manicure every week. And bought her clothes someplace not Walmart. She scooped Spider up, swung him around, set him down, and smooched his cheek. Jude got a smooch, too. But when she turned to Mom, her smile was a goner.

"What're you doing, Diamond?"

"What's it look like, Jewel?"

"I'd say you were trimming the bushes, except you haven't done that once in five years."

"Like I have time, with everything else on my plate?"

Auntie Jewel rolled her eyes, turned to Mr. Peters. "How you doing, Jim? Tolerating these August dog days?"

"The heat's hard on the grass," he said.

"If that's your biggest problem—" Mom started, but Auntie Jewel took her elbow and steered her off the driveway.

"Do not be picking fights with that man. He's just a lonesome widower with nothing to do but fuss over his lawn." Auntie Jewel tapped the toe of her shiny gold sandal. She and Uncle Hal lived two towns over. They were in real estate, meaning they owned this house and lots more places—what Auntie called "properties" and Mom called "falling down shacks."

"I am not *picking fights*. I'm sticking up for myself, same as I've had to do all my life. Unlike some spoiled people I could name."

Auntie Jewel folded her arms tight. *Tight*. Guess who had a temper evil as Mom's? The difference was, Auntie kept hers under control. Sometimes, when he was having trouble with some kid or teacher, Jude asked his aunt for advice. She'd hear him out and tell him he was right. That kid was a bully who deserved to get his butt kicked. That teacher was unfair and you better believe she knew exactly how Jude felt, because she'd had teachers like that herself. Then she'd sigh and stare up at a corner of the ceiling.

"The trick to surviving in this world," she'd say, "is making the right choice."

How were you supposed to know what the right choice was? That's what Jude couldn't figure out. Whatever choice Auntie Jewel made turned out to be the right one, but if Mom made the exact same choice, it'd probably turn out all wrong. To him it looked like it was more about the person than the choice.

"I know you're tired, Di," Auntie was telling Mom now. "I know it's not easy being a single mom. But you need to find a more positive attitude."

"And you need to stop acting like you know the first thing about being a mother, since you're not."

Auntie Jewel stiffened. Swallowed so hard Jude heard the spit going down. Spun on her high-heeled sandals and marched to her car. Spider started yipping like a puppy.

"Auntie! What'd you bring us? What'd you bring us?"

She always brought them something. Today it was the two biggest, baddest Super Soakers known to mankind.

Jude helped Spider fill his gun at the faucet on the side of the house. When he pumped it, the water shot sky high. It sparkled in the sun, making twelve million rainbows. Jude turned to grin at his mother, but the look on her face stopped him cold. Her mouth was twisted like somebody just told her she was ugly.

"I know I'm behind on the rent," she said then. "I need another week, Jewel."

"I didn't come for the rent. I came to see you and the boys." Auntie Jewel's face went soft. "Diamond, baby, why you gotta be so stubborn? You don't need to live on the edge like this. Come work for Hal and me. We'll pay you better and—"

"I'd rather take care of my old ladies than clean your old rentals, thanks anyway." Mom white-knuckled the clippers. "I'll have the rent next week, don't worry." She headed for the house.

Auntie Jewel sighed and slid her arm around Jude's shoulder.

"Be good to your mom, Jude. She needs you."

"Yeah right."

"The way people act—it's not always how they feel. And what people say—it's not always what they mean." She brushed the hair out of his eyes. "Lord. You look more like her every day."

Auntie Jewel kissed him and Spider, got in her car and drove away. When Jude turned back toward the house, his mother was assassinating his pine tree.

Gladys

The day had been grueling. The Old Woman Who Lived in a Shoe—Gladys could relate. Slumped on the front steps with the early-evening sun slanting into her eyes, she was almost too tired to squint. Out on the tree lawn, that strip of grass between the sidewalk and the street, cicadas buzzed in the tree branches. Dada said where he grew up, they called those slices of grass "devil strips," and those bugs really did sound like something out of you-know-where.

Sophie was flinging herself around, pretending she could do cartwheels. Her mother was late for pickup, as usual.

"Watch me," Sophie commanded. "Say, *Wow!* Say, *Sophie Myers, you win the gold.*"

At least Gladys had one thing to look forward to. Her best—to be honest, her only—friend, Chickie, had promised to come over tonight. Chickie had been going to various camps all summer—science camp, tennis camp, currently cooking camp. They'd barely seen each other, and Gladys really missed her friend. Chickie appreciated Gladys's brain with its many complicated thoughts and questions about life. She herself was quiet, and she had the gift of listening.

Though lately, she'd started complaining about Gladys's vocabulary.

"You can't just say *sad* like everybody else?" she wanted to know. "You have to say *despondent*?"

"There's more than one kind of sad."

"One's enough for me," Chickie said.

Gladys peeled an Elmo sticker off her knee and rubbed the gooey patch it left behind. Maybe she was so interested in words because she hadn't talked till she was almost three years old, when to everyone's astonishment she'd suddenly said, "My feet hurt." The social worker discovered she had blisters from wearing shoes several sizes too small, and it was time for a new foster home.

Maybe she was just trying to make up for lost time. She rubbed her knee. Maybe—

"Watch me do a headstand!" shrieked Sophie, bucking like a wild pony. "Say, *Sophie, you are the best in the whole uniworse!*" She toppled over, then scrambled up and ran to huddle against Gladys. "Who's that?"

Gladys followed her stare.

The woman and her dog! They were trudging by for the second time today, this time in the opposite direction. A cigarette hung from the corner of the woman's mouth. Her shirt, Gladys saw, was inside out. Her limp hair had a purple streak, like a streamer left over from a long-ago party.

"Dog," Sophie whispered, pointing.

"Yes."

"Spooky lady."

"Hush!"

The cicadas fell silent. The woman stuttered to a stop. She threw down her cigarette and ground it with her dirty sneaker. She wasn't old, but her face was stiff as a wooden mask. When

17

the cigarette was good and dead she pulled out her phone and began to scroll. And scroll. Her thumb assaulted the screen, her forehead puckering, her frown deepening. Once again she seemed to completely forget the sweet dog on the end of the leash.

That dog! She—Gladys was suddenly one hundred percent certain the dog was a girl and Gladys always trusted her intuitions—she was gazing into the distance again. Her look was sad yet patient, and something about it pried open a dark space deep inside Gladys. When the dog turned, their eyes met. She was close enough that Gladys could see those eyes were blue. The truest blue she'd ever seen.

They held each other's gaze. Wordless communication flew between them.

I'm looking for someone, the dog said.

I know, Gladys said, and the words echoed through the dark space inside her. *I know*.

The next two things happened at the exact same time. Mama opened the front door and stepped outside, and the woman shoved her phone into her pocket with a look of disgust. And then, for no reason at all, she flicked her fingers at the spot between those true-blue eyes. Not just once but twice, fast and hard. The dog flinched and whimpered. Gladys gasped. As the woman shuffled away, Gladys discovered she was on her feet.

"Goodness," Mama said, taking her hand. "Who was that?"

"A witch," Sophie said.

True Blue, Gladys thought. That should be the dog's name.

"No such thing as witches, Sophie." Mama pulled Gladys down beside her on the step.

It took a moment to understand what her mother said

next. "Chickie says she's sorry but she's too tired to come over."

"What?" Gladys turned. "She called?"

"She said she tried you but you didn't pick up. She said they made Baked Alaska at camp today and it really took it out of her."

It wasn't as if Chickie was on a reality show competing against top chefs for a big-money prize. What could be tiring about camp? Camp was fun and games compared to taking care of leaky, irrational beings all day.

Plus, Gladys's phone was right beside her and she definitely had not missed a call.

"Sugar, when it rains it pours." Mama heaved a weary sigh. "Angela took a new job as a shampoo girl at the Cut 'n' Curl."

"That flake!" Gladys cried. Angela had quit before. The last time was to be a rollerblading carhop at a place across the river. "That traitor!"

"We don't call people names," Sophie said primly.

Mama folded her big hands. Her nails were bitten to the quick, a habit she was always failing to break. Gladys braced, knowing what was coming, but before Mama could speak, Sophie's mother's pickup clanked into the driveway. Mrs. Myers spouted a geyser of excuses and promised to never be late again (meaning, not till next week). Mama gave a saintly smile.

A doormat. That's what Mama was.

Gladys would have to take Angela's place as Mama's helper. It wouldn't be the first time, but this felt worse than usual. What was wrong with people anyway? How could Sophie's mother be so selfish? How could Angela leave Mama in the lurch? How could Chickie ditch her? How could anyone not love such a lovable dog?

"I'm really sorry, sugar." Mama had a big gap between her front teeth. She'd always had it, of course, but now, suddenly, the sight of it irritated Gladys. "I know you didn't plan to spend the last days of vacation stuck babysitting."

Gladys should say it was okay. Angela quitting wasn't Mama's fault, any more than that space between her teeth was. Gladys should swallow her anger and say she'd help. She ought to be kind and saintly, just like Mama.

Instead, when her mother tried to circle her with her arms, Gladys pulled away. Pretending not to see Mama's hurt look, she marched out to the tree lawn. Up in the tree, hidden in the fan-shaped leaves, the cicadas took up their devilish buzz. True Blue and her owner had disappeared again, leaving behind nothing but a murdered cigarette butt.

Jude

His mother had murdered his tree. She'd hacked it up, then bundled the branches and set them on the tree lawn for the trash truck, pretending she was a model homeowner instead of a cold-blooded killer.

Afterward, she looked like *I'm sorry* was on the tip of her tongue.

Guess where the words stayed?

Instead of apologizing, Mom drove twenty miles round trip to get Popeyes, Jude's favorite. He snapped, "I'm not hungry!" even though just the smell made him drool like a baby. He slammed the door to the room he shared with Spider and played the lame games loaded on the lame tablet the lame school had given him for the lame summer. Till Jabari texted. One word.

FORTRESS

Jude texted back one word (or was it three?).

LOL

Jabari didn't give up. He said he'd found something for the fortress and it was the chance of a lifetime but they had to act ASAP.

Jude's best friend was always putting hot sauce on his stories. Jabari's chance of a lifetime was probably nothing, and if Mom caught him sneaking out at night? Not just sneaking but sneaking across the tracks? He'd be so dead he'd be jealous of zombies.

Still.

Slipping down the hall, he peeked into the living room. Mom was zonked on the couch, her head on a doily. All their furniture was covered in doilies, which were like giant snowflakes made out of thread. Miss Edith, one of Mom's old ladies at Good Sam, made them. Whenever Mom could, she'd sit and watch Miss Edith's favorite show, *Dancing with the Stars*, with her. Not that Mom was supposed to. The administrators wanted staff on their feet at all times. But Mom said taking care of old people was more than just wiping their chins and butts.

Spider slept in the crook of her arm, thumb in his mouth, looking like the angel he wasn't, but Mom was frowning. Even in her sleep, she was mad about something.

I'm on 2nd, Jabari texted.

On my way

When he got to Second Street, he found Jabari waiting in front of a house that looked like it had puked out its insides. Chairs, tables, boxes of dishes, garbage bags stuffed with clothes and shoes and who knows what. Everything was worn out and beat-up except for one thing. It rose out of the rubble like a giant white tombstone:

"Beautyrest," Jabari said, tapping the label. "My gram says that's the best you can buy."

The mattress was still wrapped in plastic, like whoever got evicted didn't get the chance to sleep on it even once. Jude bet they hated to leave it behind. Jabari started listing all the ways they could use it in their fortress.

"A bed, yeah. But also a wall or a shield. Jude Dude! I saw this video where a guy shoots up a mattress with an assault rifle. It doesn't stop the bullets, but it slows them down."

Calling Jabari skinny didn't begin to cover it. His biceps

were the size of olives. Plus he had a big birthmark down one side of his face. Bully bait, all right, and Jude was always having to take up for him, another reason he hated school.

Who knew mattresses were this freaking heavy? They tried carrying it over their heads, then under their arms, then dragging it. A man driving by tried to clown them. *Running away from home?* Jude was embarrassed, but Jabari hardly noticed. He was on task, as their teachers would say. Eyes on the prize.

Train whistle—two long, one short, one more long. They had to wait at the tracks, near Freddy's. The smell of burgers and fries made Jude's empty stomach weep. Jabari poked him in his arm.

"JD, can I tell you something?"

"No."

"You are the definition of ripe."

"I'm ripe, you're rotten."

"I want to tell you about this invention called deodorant."

"I want to tell you about this operation called a head transplant."

Once the train was past, they crossed the tracks.

No-man's-land. Grain mill, scrapyard, canning factory. Empty fields, empty houses. At the beginning of the summer, Jude and Jabari had scouted around till they found the perfect location. The abandoned house had a pointy roof like little kids drew. A silver maple, not doing too good, out front, and a rickety wooden fence running along one side of the yard. The closest house looked like it was abandoned, too. *Perfect.*

Up the driveway to the backyard, where they finally dropped the mattress.

"Water," croaked Jabari, a man dying in the desert. "Water!"

Inside, the house smelled bad, but not as bad as you'd think. Somehow the town had never got around to boarding the place up or cutting off the water. Jude and Jabari wrestled each other for a drink, sticking their heads under the kitchen faucet and taking big gulps before going back outside.

The fortress was amazing if Jude said so himself. Three walls were built from stuff they'd found. They'd used the fence for a fourth side. The roof was a cool camouflage tarp. They peeled that back, then tried to shove the mattress in. It was like wrestling a massive slice of cheese. When they finally got the thing in, they flopped down on their backs, worn out and happy.

The sky looked like somebody spilled crushed ice across a black table.

And it was quiet. Some crickets. The crinkle of the plastic on the mattress. Train whistles, of course. But mostly it was like a giant held up his hands, ordering the rest of the world, *Hush. Keep it down.*

Looking at the stars made Jude remember his father pointing upward, telling him to make a wish. Maybe he remembered it. The pictures in his head were like random pages torn out of a book. A man tucked him in, singing about three little birds. Leaned over Jude's bed, the rays of the ceiling light bending around him. In a yellow kitchen, a man held out a spoonful of warm rice pudding. His mother was laughing, singing that old Beatles song about Jude.

When his father got killed in action overseas, Jude was four. All he remembered about that was Mom crying.

Mom.

Jude sat up. Jabari was saying how next they needed electricity. He'd seen a YouTube on how to build your own generator.

"Time to bounce," Jude interrupted. "My mother catches me..."

He didn't have to finish that sentence. Jabari knew Mom.

They pulled the tarp back in place. Walking home, Jabari said once they had electricity, they could get a fridge. A little one, like his sister took to college. Jabari! He was always pumped over some new idea. Most of them were straight-up ridiculous, but now and then he struck gold. He could drive Jude loco, but mostly he didn't know what he'd do without his friend.

At Jabari's corner they did their secret handshake, then Jude started running. He was a trash runner, and by the time he got home he had a killer stitch in his side. At the back door he stopped to catch his breath. Through the next-door window he saw Mr. Peters in his button-down shirt, vacuuming. Didn't the dude ever give it a rest?

Jude held his breath, eased the door open. For once, luck was on his side. Mom and Spider were still zonked on the couch.

• • •

Later, when Mom carried Spider in and tucked him into the other bed, Jude squeezed his eyes tight and held his breath again. Mom was a walking lie detector. What if she could smell the outdoors on him? What if she could hear his heart thudding?

She bent close. Smoothed his hair. A touch so gentle, he almost opened his eyes to see her. He listened to her tiptoe out, shut the door behind her.

Rolling over, he watched Spider sleep. Face mashed in the pillow, arm hanging down. Did all little kids sleep that hard or was it just Spy?

If he had X-ray vision he could look up and see the stars, like at the fortress.

He listened to his brother snuffle like a furry animal in its burrow. Touched the spot where his mother had smoothed his hair. At last he fell asleep.

He dreamed they lived in the fortress. Him and Spider. There might have been a dog, too. It was a good dream.

Gladys

Waiting to fall asleep was like crossing a bridge where you didn't know what you'd find on the other side. When she was first adopted, Gladys had so many bad dreams she slept with her parents every night. She'd wake up crying, only to find them right there, Dada peacefully snoring and Mama wide awake, as if she hadn't shut her eyes all night but instead kept watch, fending off the toothy monsters, the rising waters, the raging fires, the other children who tried to bury Gladys alive.

Gladys Gladys Gladys, Mama would whisper. *You make us so glad glad glad.*

Her name was the only thing she had from her birth mother, who'd lost Gladys to foster care when she was one, then died of an overdose before Gladys was two. She'd named Gladys after herself. Mama said that proved she'd loved her baby girl with all her heart and every ounce of her being.

This was the kind of thing Mama said.

Tonight Gladys tossed and turned, flipping her pillow to the cool side, taking calming breaths, till at last she gave up and went to the window. Looking down, to her astonishment she saw True Blue all alone on the tree lawn. The dog's eyes shone like blue Christmas lights, and when she spied Gladys she whimpered piteously, begging for help. Had she run away? Was she lost? Gladys pushed up the screen and leaned out. Now she saw the leash was hooked to a branch of the tree. Only it wasn't a branch. It was a human arm covered with bark. Set in the tree trunk was a small, creepy mouth that opened and closed, making horrible, garbled sounds. True Blue's owner had turned into a tree! The dog whined in fear as the tree-mouth struggled to say something Gladys couldn't hear but knew was *Save me! Save me, please!* Gladys leaned out farther, only she leaned too far and . . .

Gladys bolted up in bed, heart thudding.

The nightmare was so real, it took all her courage to make herself get up and look out the window. There was the tree, the empty tree lawn, the sky brimming with stars. Here she was, both feet on her bedroom floor, yet she could still feel herself falling . . .

Gladys spun away from the window and went to the stand Dada had built for her dictionary. With shaky hands, she gripped the edges of the book which, when she got it for her eighth birthday, had weighed nearly as much as she did. Gladys had begged for a real dictionary. Not the baby kind they had at school, with words everybody already knew, but one with every word in the English language. The book that Mama and Dada gave her contained over 500,000 definitions.

Its pages were thin as tissue paper, but durable, which was a good thing, since Gladys had spent countless hours turning them. She did it now, one page after another, till, little by little, she began to feel better. Words. There was a word for everything that existed. That was so comforting. Once you could name something, you owned it, in a way. You possessed a kind of power over it. Whatever that thing was, it couldn't confuse or scare you, not once you knew its definition.

Gladys wanted to know all the words.

Jude

"Did you do your summer reading yet?" Mom's finger was two inches from his nose.

"Uh...gotta get the book. I meant to get it, but—"

"Why is every word out of your mouth a sorry excuse, Jude? School's around the corner. You want to have another bad year? You want to get held back again? Is that what you want?"

She was jamming her feet into her work shoes. Mom's feet swelled and her back ached and her hands knotted up, but she never missed a shift at Good Sam.

"I'll try to get the book today," he said. "But—"

"The only *but* I want is your butt in gear. I can't do everything myself. When I get home the laundry better be done. And your brother better not be parked in front of the TV screen like a freaking mushroom." She hoisted the massive purse. "What about your math review?"

"Okay, I will, I—"

"I am not playing with you, Jude. I am so not..."

Still scolding, she barreled out the door.

No pine branches to whap her today.

Spider used to go to the daycare near Good Sam. The teachers were always telling Mom how he had poor impulse control. Like she didn't already know that? The teachers were too dumb to understand a kid like Spy. Why pay good money for that? As soon as vacation started, she pulled him out. Guess who became Daycare Central?

Jude made his bed and Spider's, then went down the basement to start a load of laundry. When he got to the kitchen he found Spider sitting on top of the refrigerator drawing in the dust. Once Jude got him down, he tried to make his baby brother sing the ABCs with him. But Spy wanted to watch *Thomas*, a show that ranked with the lamest of the lame. Trains that talked with accents? For real? But it kept Spider out of trouble, at least for a while. Jude finished the laundry and was making lunch when his phone pinged with a text.

Jabari: *Meet u know where*

Jude: *Stuck with tarantula*

Jabari: *Bring him*

Keeping secrets from Mom made Jude's life easier. Most of his secrets were small, but the fortress—that was big. *Big.* Mom had a serious thing about the other side of the tracks. Coyotes, wild dogs, rats, not to mention dopeheads. They stole stuff from abandoned buildings. Got high there, sometimes OD'd there. Last winter the cops found a frozen-stiff body behind a grain silo.

Jabari said dopeheads were mostly just stupid, nothing to stress about. But that wasn't true. Spider's Dad, Holden? He wasn't stupid, at least not when he first moved in with them. He worked in a restaurant. He taught Jude how to make killer grilled cheese. How to play chess. Gave him the tree guide. Holden told Jude he should go out for football. Teased him about how one day he'd break all the fine girls' hearts, even though Jude was scared of both football and fine girls.

Then Holden got hurt in that car accident. He started

taking drugs for the pain. And then, Mom said, the drugs took him. She gave him a bunch of chances, then kicked him out.

The last time they saw Holden was when he showed up uninvited for Spider's third birthday party. High as a skyscraper. Uncle Hal escorted him out while Auntie Jewel informed him that if he ever—ever—showed his sorry, punked-out, lying, thieving self within a mile of this house, she'd personally run him over. A smear on the blacktop, that's what would be left of Holden.

He must've believed her. They hadn't seen or heard from him since.

One night not long after the party, Spider had a bad dream. When Jude climbed into his bed with him, Spider snuggled close. "Daddy," he said, voice all small and choky. *I'm not*, Jude almost said. But didn't.

Now Spider barreled into the kitchen and got busy tearing the crusts off his sandwich. Spider didn't talk about Holden anymore. When you were little, you forgot stuff. It slid away, like scenery out a car window. At least Jude hoped that's what had happened for Spider.

Jude finished his sandwich. Picked up the house keys. Jiggled them. Put them back down. He went to the front window and looked at his snuffed-out pine tree. Mom would freak if she knew he'd been hanging out across the tracks. If she found out he took Spider there?

On a scale from 1 to 10 of bad situations, disobeying her could be a straight up 10. But another day cooped up in this house? A definite 15.

Besides, he and Jabari had already gone there twelve million times and nothing bad ever happened. He picked up his phone and texted Jabari.

On our way

Gladys

That morning, Gladys pulled on shorts and a tee, then opened her closet. After careful deliberation, she chose a silver taffeta capelet she'd found at Aunt Annie's Attic. To compensate for wearing clothes designed for third graders, Gladys often wore vintage accessories from the thrift shop. She had a collection of hats, shoes, and costume jewelry that she hoped signaled a sense of style and sophistication. Usually she wouldn't waste those things on the sprouts, but today she needed a boost.

Before she went downstairs she looked out her window. The tree lawn tree stood innocently in the sun.

Mama had already taken the sprouts outside. In the kitchen, Dada, wearing boots, baggy pants, and goofy suspenders, yawned as he filled his extra-large travel mug with steaming coffee. This summer he'd managed to find work at Crooked River Farm and Village, a re-creation of rural life in the 1800s. He worked in the gift shop, selling hand-dipped candles and stuffed cows and sheep. Setting the top on his mug, he yawned again. Back when he'd worked at the auto plant, Dada was never tired. He was proud. He'd bragged about how they rolled out over eight thousand new cars a day. *Eight thousand* and they could hardly keep up with the demand! Dada thought he'd work there forever, but instead here he was, forced to wear a hat shaped like an upside down flower pot.

He took one look at Gladys and poured her some coffee, heavy on the cream and sugar.

"Looks like somebody else is having trouble getting started today," he said, handing it to her. To look more 1800-ish, he'd grown a beard. A terrible mistake if you asked Gladys. Though the hair on his head was thick black curls, the beard came in dark-red and patchy, and even if you loved him, it was impossible to call those bristles attractive.

Plus, it itched. He scratched it now with his wide brown fingers, then clinked her mug with his.

"Thanks for helping Mama. Without you, she'd be in big time trouble."

On cue, Sophie barreled into the kitchen. Her nose was a snot faucet, and she delicately wiped it on Gladys's taffeta capelet. Kids with green snot were supposed to stay home. Dada pulled a cloth handkerchief from the pocket of his breeches and swiped Sophie's revolting nose. He grabbed his mug and took his keys off the hook. When he spoke again, he used his Crooked River Farm and Village voice.

"I fear I'm expected at my establishment, gentle ladies. Would you do me the favor of excusing me?" He tipped his hat, bowed, and left.

Sophie said, "That's your father."

Sprouts needed to state facts, even obvious ones, as if to make sure that what was true yesterday still held true today. The world was so new to them, they thought anything could happen anytime. Up could become down, wrong could become right, that man with the kindly face and silly hat might not be Dada but a total stranger.

Through the kitchen door screen, Gladys watched her father kiss Mama goodbye and drive away. Her parents claimed that the moment they met Gladys, they knew they were meant to be a family. But how could they have known? She was only three, younger than Sophie. Barely human yet, hardly even speaking. How could they have known what she'd be like when she had a mind of her own with a million thoughts, and questions she couldn't answer, and words, lots and lots of words? How could they be sure, back when she was little, that they'd always love her?

The nightmare crept back, giving Gladys a shiver. If she told Mama, her mother would say, *It's just a dream, let it go.* Mama was expert at comforting, scattering scary stuff the way little Lily was scattering dandelion fluff now. Starry seeds drifted about, lifting on the breeze.

"Make a wish!" Gladys heard Mama tell Lily. "Wish for something wonderful!"

It was just a dream, but it was Gladys's dream. She couldn't share it with Mama. She wasn't sure why, but she couldn't. She wouldn't.

Gladys felt a tug on her capelet. She looked down into nostrils oozing green slime.

"Are you upset?"

"Tissue, Sophie."

"Don't keep your upset inside."

"What?"

"Ms. Suza says that. She's your mother."

Jude

Jude told Spider they were going someplace magic. If Spider breathed a word to anyone, especially—*especially*—their mother, the place would disappear. Spider bought it. He took his Super Soaker, and by the time they got to the fortress, he'd shot dead a mess of cars, squirrels, trees, cats, and other little kids. He tried to shoot up a bench of old men but one of them knocked the gun away with his cane, quick as a Ninja assassin.

As they walked up the house's driveway, brown grasshoppers busted out of the tall grass. Bees hummed in the flowers tumbling over the fence. Usually bees freaked Spider out, but he was too excited to notice. When Jude showed him the fortress, though, he looked confused.

"That's magic?" he asked.

Jabari was already there, straining his nonexistent muscles to drag a massive board from behind the garage.

"Help me, JD," he grunted. "Watch the nails."

Killer nails stuck out all over the board. It would've made a great weapon if it didn't weigh as much as a baby elephant. Jabari said it'd make their fortress 100 percent impenetrable. By the time they'd dragged it across the yard, Spider was inside the fortress. When Jude checked, his baby brother looked up, all bug-eyed.

"It is magic," he said.

"Told you."

"I'm making a wish."

Jude almost laughed. Or cried. Or something. "For what?"

Spider didn't answer. He got busy lining up pebbles and twigs on the Beautyrest. Whispering to himself, something about a train going into outer space. Jude had to smile. Maybe he hadn't been lying. This place *was* magic. When you came here, you got lifted out of the real world and set down someplace where you were a different, better version of yourself. Jabari wasn't bully bait—he was in charge. Spider was contented. He was…what? Easier. Not mad, not worried. Jude almost wished their mother could see them now. See what Jude had built and how good Spider was behaving. Maybe she'd be a little proud.

Yeah right.

Do not even think about her.

Jude grabbed Spider's Super Soaker and went inside the house. He filled the gun under the kitchen faucet. Some kid had crayoned his name on the wall. TED. The E had like ten lines instead of three. Jude bet Ted got in big trouble for writing on the wall.

Outside, Jabari was bending over, butt in the air. Perfect ambush position! Jude's finger was on the trigger when he heard a scream that took his scalp off.

"Bees! Bees!"

Spider busted out of the fortress. His eyes were shut and he was slapping the air with both hands.

"Spy! Look out!"

Too late. Spider tripped. Sucked in a breath, his mouth a hole, and fell over sideways. In slow motion and high definition, it seemed like, so Jude could see the big nail waiting to poke his eye out.

Spider let out a howl like a black wind.

"They stinged me!"

For a wild second Jude hoped it was true. Spider had gotten stung and was freaking out—that was all. Then he saw the cut. Spider's eye was still in his head, but just above it, a jagged cut poured down blood.

And more blood.

"Spidey. It's okay." Jude wiped it with his T-shirt. "You're okay, Spy!"

"Here!" Jabari came running with some gray stuff. "Spider-web. Gram says it stops bleeding."

"Are you whack? Get that away from him!"

"I'm blooding!" screamed Spider. "I'm dying!"

"Suck it," Jabari told Jude.

"What?!"

"To get the poison out."

Jude was pretty sure that's what you did for snakebites, not puncture wounds, but he put his lips to his little brother's head and sucked. The salty taste of blood filled his mouth. Spider, weirdest kid on planet Earth, laughed.

"That tickles," he said, then cried even harder. "I want Mom!"

Desperate, Jude took the sticky web and patted it on the cut.

"Did he have his shots?" Jabari wanted to know.

"What?" Jude couldn't believe how calm Jabari was. Either he didn't get that this was the last day of Jude's life or he didn't care.

"You know. The shots you get when you're a baby. One's for tetanus. The disease you get from rusty nails."

Wasn't getting a hole ripped in your flesh bad enough? You

could get a disease, too? Jude looked at the nails sticking out of the board. Rusty. Rusty for sure.

Jabari pulled out his phone and read out loud the tetanus symptoms. Fever. Tightening of the jaw. Swelling. Difficulty swallowing...

"Shut up!" said Jude.

Jabari looked surprised. Even a little hurt. "He probably got his shots," he said. "You probably don't have to worry."

Spider was doing that gulping thing that happens when you cry yourself dry. As far as Jude could tell, his jaw looked normal. But blood was smeared all over his face, his hair, his hands. Jude would've given anything to reverse time and put his little brother back inside the fortress, making his magic train, acting so sweet you loved him with no problem.

"He might need stitches though," Jabari said. "The time my sister split her head open on the coffee table—"

"Guess what?" Jude exploded. "This would've never happened except for you. I told you we shouldn't bring him but you talked me into it. Same with that freaking board. This whole thing was your jerk-face idea."

Jabari stared, confused. He really did look sorry, and for some reason, that made Jude even madder. With strength he didn't know he had, he picked up the board and threw it. It knocked a sheet of plywood sideways, then kept on going, flattening a corner of the fortress and dragging off the tarp.

"Look what you did!" Stupid Jabari looked like he might stupid cry. "What'd you do that for?"

"This fort was the world's lamest idea!"

"It's a fortress."

"The only thing lamer is you!"

"You didn't have to wreck it!"

"Shut your face before I do it for you!"

Jude was afraid his brother might refuse to walk, but he let Jude take his hand.

"Why are you blaming me?" Jabari yelped. "It was an accident. It's nobody's fault he got hurt."

Jabari knew nothing. *Nothing.*

Jabari kept calling after them, but guess who refused to turn around?

Gladys

If there was one thing sprouts hated more than going to sleep it was being woken up. After-nap was a cranky, crabby time and Gladys was overjoyed when her father, who'd only worked a short shift today, came home and took her place helping Mama. Grabbing her phone, she sat on her bed playing Scrabble till she knew Chickie would be home from camp.

"I have volumes to tell you," she said when Chickie picked up. "I hardly know where to start!"

"Hi, Gladys."

"Can I come over?"

"Sure."

"On my way!"

Gladys took off her capelet and hung it back in the closet. She had too much to tell her best friend to waste time explaining her fashion preferences, which Chickie had recently begun to question, along with Gladys's vocabulary.

Dada offered to drive her, but Gladys said she'd ride her bike. The bike was the kind that comes with training wheels, though of course she didn't need those anymore. It was impossible to get up any speed on the thing. Also, her parents, afraid cars wouldn't see her despite the humiliating flag mounted on the back, made her ride on the sidewalk.

Still! Freedom! She reveled in the feel of the wind in her

hair. Or at least on her helmet. She bumped over the sidewalk, lifted and broken by the roots of tree lawn trees. As she pedaled past one with a crosswise crack in the trunk, whoosh! The black mist of her nightmare blew around her. Bad dreams were supposed to evaporate in daylight, but this one refused.

Shuddering, she bent her head and pedaled harder. She'd tell Chickie about the tree-woman crying *Save me! Save me, please!* Chickie would give the dream the respect it deserved. She'd listen attentively as Gladys described sweet True Blue and her witchy owner. She'd grow irate over how Angela had quit again, leaving Gladys mired in the quicksand of daycare.

Gladys hoped she wouldn't burst before she had the chance to tell her best friend absolutely everything. Sweat trickled down from under her helmet and stung her eyes, so she didn't even notice the two boys walking toward her until the tall one cried, "Watch where you're going!"

Gladys hit the brakes. She was prepared to be indignant— her bicycle skills were excellent—till she got a closer look. The tall one—everyone was tall to Gladys, but he was extra tall—she recognized. Big as he was, he was a grade behind her. He and Gladys had never spoken. Besides being in a different grade, and a boy, he was not what anyone would call friendly. Before today, if she'd had to describe him in a single word, she'd have chosen *sullen*.

Now, though, she added *handsome*. Sullenly handsome. He had blond curls and a high, intelligent brow. Which was as sweaty as hers, but somehow this made him look gallant, like a knight who'd been out slaying dragons. Was that blood on his T-shirt?

Gladys fanned her overheated face.

The sprout had something filmy and gray—it almost looked like a spiderweb—stuck to a nasty cut on his forehead. His face was *definitely* streaked with blood and his hair was clumped with it.

"Are you all right?" The most obtuse question possible. "I mean, can I help you?"

The little boy lay down on the tree lawn and abruptly went as stiff as a corpse with rigor mortis.

"Get up," said the other one.

Jude, thought Gladys. She was pretty sure she'd heard him called Jude. From his tone of voice, she guessed the two were brothers.

"Spider," he begged. "There's dog crap. Come on. Get up."

"The gun," Spider moaned. "We forgot the gun."

"Gun?" Gladys said, but they both ignored her.

"It's okay, Spy. I'll get it later."

Compared to his brother, Spider was scrawny. Also, his hair was straight and dark instead of blond and wavy. They didn't, in fact, look anything like brothers, but Jude definitely acted like one. He acted like a dad, almost. Gladys watched him try to pick up Spider, who continued to do his imitation of a plank.

"Help me out here," Jude pleaded, and even though Gladys knew he was talking to Spider, she was the one who answered.

"Do you want to borrow my bike? You could ride him home."

He eyed her, then the bike, and for a second she thought he was going to laugh.

"Maybe if I was six years old."

"Oh. Right. Well, I can ride him."

"Really?" He considered it, then shook his head. "Forget it. It's going to take a bulldozer to move him."

Gladys crouched beside Spider. "You can wear my bike helmet," she whispered in his ear.

Spider lifted his head and side-eyed her neon-pink helmet.

"Deal," he whispered back.

Gladys took the helmet off her head and set it on his, careful with the cut. Jude watched in astonishment. Astonishment transformed his handsomeness into cuteness.

"I never met a sprout who could resist a helmet," Gladys told him as she climbed back onto her bike.

"We live on Church Street." When Jude set Spider onto the bike seat, the little boy wrapped his arms around Gladys's middle and pressed his cheek against her spine.

Gladys never rode helmet-less, and though it made her nervous, it also felt daring and bold. She stood on the pedals as Jude jogged beside them, over the bumps in the sidewalk, in and out of lawn sprinklers. The edge of a paperback stuck out of his back pocket. That was interesting. She kept waiting for him to say something, anything, but he seemed to be a person of few words. Also, a terrible runner.

As they approached Church Street, Gladys slowed down, suddenly in no hurry to get there. That was when she registered the woman ahead on the sidewalk, standing still, her back toward them. With a cry, Gladys braked, but Jude, head bent, huffing and puffing, plowed directly into her. Down they both fell in a horrible heap of cries and grunts and a pitiful yelp from True Blue, who'd been sitting patiently and now was on the bottom of the pile.

"Good God!" yelled the woman. Plus other inappropriate phrases.

True Blue wriggled out and tried to back away, but her leash was wrapped around the woman's leg. Struggling to get free, the dog twisted this way and that, tossing her head, growling and yipping as the choke collar tightened and she grew more and more frantic.

"It's gonna bite you!" Spider looked terrified. "Jude! Don't let it bite you!" Waving his arms, he catapulted off the bike and crashed helmet-first to the sidewalk.

True Blue started barking. It was a piercing, scraping sound, like a shovel at the bottom of a bucket. A bucket of metal scraps. Her sides heaved and her eyes bulged. Scrambling to his feet, Jude reached for the twisted leash, and Gladys saw he was as scared as his little brother. Yet somehow he managed to untangle True Blue, and when he stepped back onto the grass, she immediately stopped barking and went still. She sat at his feet, tail neatly wrapped around her. She and Jude looked at each other, both of them breathing too hard.

The woman was peering around in a confused way, like someone who'd just gotten very bad news. When she spied her phone on the sidewalk, she snatched it and hauled herself upright.

"Look what you did!" She stuck the phone in Jude's frightened face. "It's cracked! Ruined!"

This was definitely not the woman from Gladys's nightmare. The dream woman was helpless and voiceless, but this one screeched like a bird of prey.

"Sorry." Jude took a step back, and True Blue scooted behind him.

"Sorry? Sorry!" She was getting angrier by the second. She shoved the phone in his face again. "Like sorry fixes anything? Like sorry means *crap*?"

Why didn't Jude defend himself? Gladys two-footed her bike closer.

"It's not his fault!" she cried. "It was an accident! We were in a hurry. His little brother's hurt."

The woman turned to look at Spider, sitting in a heap on the ground. Blood trickled through the gray stuff and down his cheek. Her cruel eyes widened.

"What happened to *him*?"

"That's what I'm trying to tell you," Gladys said.

"That kid needs stitches. What is the matter with you little punks?" She pulled a pack of cigarettes from her pocket but it was crushed. She jammed it back in, then whipped the leash out of Jude's hand. True Blue gave a desperate bark and the woman smacked her snout with the phone.

"Don't do that!" Gladys cried. "You hurt her! Why did you do that?"

Whatever evil lived inside the woman vanished. Or maybe—maybe whatever goodness she possessed rose to the surface. For a second, she looked ashamed of herself.

But only for a second.

"You brats owe me a phone. Who are your parents? Where do you live? Never mind—get out of here! Get out of my sight before I . . ." She pointed at Spider, who was crying without making any noise. "Take care of that pathetic kid! And you better pray I never see you again or I'll . . . I'll . . ." She stepped into the street, yanking True Blue after her. "You heard me!"

The woman had the leash in a death grip, but as they

crossed the street, True Blue managed to twist her head. Jude turned his own head away, and Gladys understood why. He couldn't stand to look.

She wiped Spider's tears with a tissue from her pocket, then helped him back onto the bike. They'd gone several blocks before Jude said a word.

"If I was him," he said, his hands balled into fists, "I'd run away."

"It's a girl."

"How do you know?"

"I just do."

"Well I just know it's a boy."

"Girl."

"Boy."

"Girl."

"Boy."

"Anyway you're right. It's terrible," Gladys said. "It's worse than terrible. It's heartbreaking. It's criminal. It's—"

"Here's our house."

What? Already?

Jude lifted his brother down.

"I think he really does need stitches," Gladys said.

Which made Jude scowl, as if she was criticizing him instead of offering helpful advice. He wrestled the bike helmet off Spider and shoved it toward her.

"Thanks."

"You're welcome. By the way, my name is Gladys."

He was carrying his brother toward the door, which had a menacing totem pole, or something, beside it.

"I live on Fifth Street," she called. "The yellow house with kid stuff all over the place."

Without so much as a glance back, he shut the door behind them.

"Goodbye," she said to the empty air.

A moment passed. Gladys's legs were trembly and her chest ached. She had a vague feeling that there was something she was supposed to do, yet she didn't move. Next door, a man came outside wearing giant kneepads. He knelt in the grass, every blade of which was precisely the same height, and began to weed a perfect-looking flower bed. Though Gladys had heard the expression *neat as a pin*, she'd never known what it meant till now. Pins were spare, no-nonsense things. Nothing comforting about a pin. The yard should have been nice, but somehow it made Gladys feel sorry for the man, his grass, even his kneepads.

Looking back at Jude's front door, which remained shut, she remembered his face as he gazed at True Blue. *Stricken*, she thought. People could be stricken with illness or sorrow, but also with love.

She slowly put her bike helmet back on. As if that jolted her brain, she remembered. Chickie! She'd promised to be at her house at least an hour ago.

Flag flying, she furiously pedaled back the way she'd just come.

Jude

It wasn't his fault, Auntie Jewel said when he called her. Jude was too young to have full responsibility for a four-year-old, especially one who needed as much supervision as Spider. She said Jude was a good brother who did his best.

Jude knew she was just trying to make him feel better. He wanted her to. Why else did he call her, instead of Mom at work? Auntie Jewel showed up, took one look at Spider, and put them both in her car. On the way to the emergency room, Jude told her about the rusty nail and watched her go even paler.

He'd done the smart thing, calling her right away, she said.

Only he hadn't called her right away. He'd waited till he realized the blood was never going to stop unless Spider stayed still, and no way that was going to happen. By then Jude was so scared it took three tries to tap in Auntie's number.

Even when the ER nurse gave Spider something to calm him down. Even when it still took two more nurses to hold him while the doctor did the stitches. Even when his mother showed up, having ten heart attacks. Even when Jude gave Mom the short version of what had happened and she fixed her eyes on him in a way that made his stomach twist like he'd swallowed a snake. Even then, Auntie Jewel kept saying it wasn't his fault.

"Jude called me right away," she told Mom.

"There's a reason you have my work number in your phone,

Jude." Mom did that thing where she talked without opening her mouth. "You know that, right?"

Afterward, in the hospital garage, Mom couldn't remember where she'd parked. She aimed her key around, trying to make her car beep. By the time they found it, nobody was talking. With a sad-eyed look, Auntie Jewel got in her car and drove away.

Jude sat in the back with Spider, who fell asleep right away. Jude stared out the window, his brain doing the Tilt-A-Whirl. That girl and her dinky excuse for a bike. In second grade, his class had a gerbil that ran around its wheel like that. He'd noticed that girl at school. Weird clothes, a face that was too pointy. When she took off her bike helmet, her hair sprang out like the rays of the sun, if the sun was brown.

The way she stood up to that fossil lady!

What did she say her name was? Something old-timey, like one of Mom's Good Sam ladies.

He kept seeing Spooky, twisting around to look back at them. He kept trying to un-see it.

Mom pulled into the driveway. Opened the car door and picked up Spider. Feeling sick, Jude followed them to the front door. Standing next to what was left of his pine tree, he watched her put her key in the lock.

"I shouldn't have taken him there," he said.

No reply.

"I'm sorry. I swear I won't do it again."

His mother laid Spider on the couch. Jude kept an eye on her hands, ready to dodge. But they just hung at her sides like iron weights.

"I'm taking a shower," she said. "Watch him."

After her shower she cooked dinner—real dinner, chicken

and biscuits from scratch. Jude couldn't remember the last time she made biscuits. He should've been too upset to eat but he was starving. He kept waiting for her to tell him to quit hogging the food, but she didn't even seem to notice. When Spider wouldn't eat anything, she let him have ice cream. Two big bowls.

She gave Spider a sponge bath. Got him in his PJs, fed him some medicine, and put him in her bed. Read him a story off her phone, then lay with him till he fell asleep. By the time she got a beer from the fridge and came back to the living room, the quiet had lasted so long Jude was ready to jump out of his skin. He was trying to decide if he should lead off with another apology, but she spoke first.

"My sister says I depend on you too much." She popped the beer, took a sip. "But she doesn't know you like I do. She's your aunt. I'm your *mother*." Another sip. "You're smart, Jude. You know what's what."

People always said his mother was pretty. Sometimes, like now, when she was wearing her pink hoodie and the curls weren't ironed out of her hair, he thought so, too. He couldn't help looking at the scar on her lip, though. Would Spider have a scar? His mother took another sip of beer, and after a few beats she spoke again.

"You're smart," she repeated. "You get that from your dad. He was the most intelligent person I ever met. If he'd lived, there's no telling what he could've done. That's why you making these bad decisions…" She looked away. "It just breaks my heart. You could do so much better, Jude. You have so much potential. I know your brother's a handful. He's got issues. But he looks up to you."

Jude picked up a doily, balled it in his fist. If Spider got a scar, it would be all his fault. She took another sip.

"I won't have you ending up like me, stuck in this dead-end town. You're going to college. You're going places."

"Mom," he tried. "You're smart, too. You could go back to school or—"

"Don't change the subject, mister." She peered past him like she saw something in the distance. But it must have disappeared because she sat up straight and rolled her shoulders. "We're talking about you. The way you screwed up today, no way I should trust you again. But you can do better. I know it, and I think you know it, too."

When Jude swallowed, it was like sharp stones scraped his throat.

"Spider," he said. "He liked it there. He was having fun before—"

"Spider is four years old. He's got less sense than a cupcake. You're lucky nothing worse happened! Do not get me started again! You go anywhere near that so-called fortress and I will not be responsible for my actions. Do you hear me, Jude?"

He nodded, not looking at her.

"We're calling this a reset," she said. "A new start. You're grounded, that goes without saying. But you're going to use the time to study, every single day. No way you're getting bad grades another year. And I'm making a to-do list. We're going to work together to fix up this dump, starting with the bathroom."

Down the hall in her room, Spider started whimpering. Mom stood up. Jude could feel her eyes on him, but still he didn't look at her. After a moment she sank back down beside him.

"Look at me." She took his chin, turned his face toward her. "You think I like talking to you this way? You think I want to be lecturing and punishing you? I don't. I love you and your brother.

I'm doing everything I can for us, but I can't do it all. I need your help. I got to count on you."

Her eyes were shiny with tears. She pulled his head against her shoulder and held it there.

"I love you up to the moon and stars," she whispered. "I want to be proud of you. Make me proud of you, okay?"

"Okay," he said. "Okay."

Gladys

Gladys jumped off her bike, ran up Chickie's front steps, and rang the bell. She was trying to catch her breath when Chickie's big sister, Annabelle, opened the door.

"Gladys! What's up?"

"Hi, Annabelle. Chickie's expecting me."

Annabelle looked confused, like Gladys was a package delivered to the wrong address.

"She's not here."

"She's not? But she knew I was coming."

Annabelle stepped onto the front porch, which had new furniture since the last time Gladys was there. The cushions were printed with crescent moons and twinkly stars.

"A girl from her camp came over. Morgan?" Annabelle said. "Do you know her?"

"I don't know anyone named Morgan."

"They were hanging around, but then they left."

"I'm late. But I thought she'd wait for me."

For a teenager, Annabelle was preternaturally nice. She gave Gladys a kindly, encouraging smile. "I think they went to Scoops. Maybe you can catch up to them."

"Thank you," Gladys said.

"You're welcome," Annabelle said, but as Gladys turned around, she gasped. "Gladys, are you all right?"

Gladys considered saying how deeply hurt her feelings were, but instead said, "Yes. Why?"

"You've got blood on your back!"

"I do? Oh yuck."

"Do you want to come in? Do you need to sit down? Not on the porch furniture—those cushions are brand-new."

"It's not *my* blood," Gladys said, which did nothing to relieve Annabelle's horrified look. Explaining seemed much too complicated, so Gladys just said goodbye and got back on her bike.

Scoops Ice Cream wasn't that far, but how could she go there wearing bloody clothes? Besides, why hadn't Chickie waited? Who was this Morgan? Chickie had never mentioned her.

She turned her bike around and slowly rode toward home. When she got to Front Street, a van was stopped at the red light. It was packed with kids, and every single one of them had sandy hair and a button nose. A sprout in a car seat waved at Gladys and Gladys automatically waved back. The sight of all those matching kids happily smooshed together made her feel like a lone tree atop a mountain. When she looked down at her sensible sneakers, which she'd worn to please Chickie, her feet seemed very far away. She'd had so much to tell her friend! Even more than she'd expected, since the encounter with Jude, not to mention seeing True Blue again. She'd pictured Chickie's jaw falling farther and farther open till it was practically unhinged.

Instead, her only true friend had ditched her for someone named Morgan.

And now she remembered how Jude had shut the door on her the minute they got to his house.

Gladys tried to be angry. She'd helped Jude, after all. Yet both he and Chickie had acted as if they couldn't care less about her.

Gladys waited for the indignation to rise inside her, but instead she just felt . . . wrong. Not wrong like she'd done something bad, but wrong like she wasn't made right.

She told herself it wasn't her fault that she had an excellent vocabulary and a unique fashion sense. It wasn't her fault that she was in the second percentile for height and that she didn't look like either of her parents. It wasn't her fault she was named after someone she couldn't remember, no matter how hard she tried.

None of those things were her fault. But suddenly, it felt as if they were.

What if there were other things wrong with her? Bigger things. Things she didn't even know about yet.

In her dream, she'd just kept falling and falling.

As the light changed and the van pulled away, the sprout in the car seat gave one last merry wave. This time Gladys didn't wave back.

Jude

When Jude woke up the next morning, he looked over at Spider, still sleeping. The bandage on his little head was like a flashing sign. LOOK WHAT MY BROTHER DID TO ME AND IT COULD HAVE BEEN WAY WORSE.

He was sorry for his brother. Sorry for throwing that board at the fortress. Sorry for the stuff he said to Jabari. He got mad every time he thought about how that lady treated Spooky and even madder knowing he'd just stood by, saying nothing. He'd done everything wrong.

Why'd that girl tell him where she lived? Like he'd ever go see her!

He wasn't going anywhere. He wasn't getting in any more trouble. No way no how. He was done messing up. Starting now, he was making all the right choices. The ones the smart kids made.

Make me proud of you, Mom begged him.

He wanted to. He wanted to up to the moon and stars.

• • •

Before she left for work, Mom handed him his orders.

- Get summer reading book
- Read book

- Practice math
- Go to hardware store

She had a list of stuff to get from the hardware store. Scraper, roller, tray, brushes, paint called Evening Dove. "Straight to the library and hardware, then straight back with every single penny of my change accounted for. Got it?"

"Got it, Mom."

Spider refused to walk unless Jude let him wear his Chucky mask from last Halloween. Why not? His brother's head already had Frankenstein stitches. It was just putting one scary face over another.

At the library, Jude didn't even look at the computers. All right, he played one game. Maybe two. But that was it. Then he got the summer reading book. Check! On to the hardware store, where Spider enjoyed spilling twelve million nails on the floor. Cleaned that up, got the painting supplies, crammed everything but the paint can into his backpack. Check! Things were going good till they started home.

"Jabari!" Spider yelled.

Jude's ex–best friend was shooting hoops at the playground with some kids from school. *Supposedly* shooting hoops. Jabari's true sports were chess and video games. When Spider yelled his name, Jabari turned around just in time for a pass to smack him in the chest and knock him on his bony butt.

"Look!" Spider whipped off the Chucky mask. "I got stitches."

Jabari scrambled to his feet as the other boys clowned him. The game started back up but he just stood there, rubbing the birthmark on the side of his face. For a second, Jude thought he'd cross the street to them. Act like nothing had happened.

"It's us," Spider called. "Me and—"

"I know who you are," Jabari said, not budging.

I didn't mean it, the fortress isn't lame, it's the opposite, I was scared, Spider's a massive pain in the butt, but if anything ever happened to him plus you know what my mother's like...

All the things Jude wanted to say tangled up in his brain. He couldn't undo the knot. Words just got him in trouble. He heard his mother saying, *Don't give me those sorry excuses. Quit trying to explain this away!*

Jabari waited another second, then slapped his hands together, spun around, and got back in the game.

Part One of that messed-up walk.

Part Two came when they turned off Front Street and Jude saw Holden. Spider's father was leaning against a porch railing, eyes closed, enjoying the sunshine.

Jude's heart turned into a piston, pumping way too fast. His hand went to the tree book, in his back pocket like always.

You're back? Guess what? I can name almost every tree in town by now. I put checks next to them. You want to see?

Holden shrugged himself upright, blinking. Shaded his eyes with his hand. He couldn't recognize Spider with the mask, but it was Jude he was looking at. Frowning like, *Am I dreaming?* He swayed a little and Jude squeezed his brother's hand so tight Spider yelped. That was when Jude realized it wasn't Holden after all. It was just some sorry dude who looked like him. Bloodshot eyes. Scooped-out face.

"Yo Chucky." He started toward them, grinning. "Yo—"

Without thinking, Jude swung the can of Evening Dove with both hands. It was heavier than he expected and the arc of it almost pulled him off his feet. The guy froze.

"Whoa. What's your problem, fella?"

Jude grabbed his brother and hauled him down the sidewalk.

"Who's that?" Spider kept twisting around, trying to see. "Who's that guy?"

"Nobody. Nobody times twelve million."

Jude felt like an idiot. The paint can banged against his leg all the way home.

Gladys

One thing about sprouts: they took your mind off everything else. Sprout-care was all about right now, this minute. No matter what disasters were going on in your life, you had to feed them and change them and make sure they didn't die from ingesting toxic substances or running into traffic. In the case of Mateo, you had to endlessly soothe him as he cut a tooth and fussed nonstop.

That afternoon, not even Mama could get Mateo to nap, so Gladys volunteered to take him for a walk. Sophie begged to come, which meant using the double stroller. Gladys set a saucer-shaped green velvet hat with a short veil on her head, tossed a lemon-colored chiffon scarf around her neck, loaded up the diaper bag, buckled the kids in, and set off.

Motion soothed unhappy sprouts. They seemed to believe life would be better somewhere else, if only they could get there. Within a block, Mateo quieted down. Sophie narrated, pointing out a red house, a white house, and a house with a car on the front lawn. When they passed a house with plywood over the windows, she wanted to know how it could see.

"Houses can't see," Gladys said.

Sophie considered this. She picked at her boogery nose. "But they can hear," she said.

"No."

"But they can talk."

"Did you ever hear a house talk, Sophie?"

"Mommy says, *If these walls could talk, the things they could tell.*"

"*If*, she says."

"When Daddy and her have a fight, she says that."

"TMI, Sophie, okay?"

The stroller weighed a ton and the sidewalks were uneven and soon her arms were ready to fall off. Mateo slumped into a sleepy heap, but Sophie twisted around to look up at Gladys.

"I have to poo," she said.

"What? Now?"

"Right now!"

"You can't wait?"

"I need to poo! The poo is coming!"

Great. Just great! Gladys unbuckled Sophie, who leaped out and started to pull down her shorts.

"Not here!" Gladys yelled. "Behind that bush!"

Her third-grade teacher lived on this street, and as Gladys stood guard she prayed Mrs. Marsh wouldn't look out her window. Though really, why were dogs allowed to poop in public but not preschoolers, who were just one step above animals themselves? Though then she'd have to carry around poop bags, which, please no. Sophie gave a loud grunt followed by a luxuriant sigh. Gladys considered handing her a tissue, imagined Sophie handing it back, and decided against it. As Sophie tugged up her shorts, her face brightened.

"I spy a doggy!"

She pointed down the block to a house with a chain-link

fence. When Gladys looked, she saw a shaggy creature pacing behind the fence.

"Can we pet it? Please, Gladys, please?"

Glady meant to say no, but an invisible force drew her closer. The yard was small, dominated by a pine tree tall and straight as the mast of a ship. In its shade sat a doghouse. Tied to it with a length of wash line . . . could it be?

"True Blue!" Gladys cried.

The dog disappeared inside her house.

"This is where you live?" Gladys's heart leaped around. "I'm so happy I found you!"

The yard was dotted with pine cones and dog turds, which looked a lot alike. A dirt track was worn from the doghouse almost to the fence. There were two bowls, both turned upside down. Gladys eyed the human house, where all the curtains were pulled tight. A couple of empty lawn chairs sat in the driveway.

"Remember me?" She put her face to the fence. "You do, I know you do."

True Blue poked her head out, but she averted her eyes. Sprouts did the same thing when they were afraid. They thought if they couldn't see you, you couldn't see them. Gladys rummaged in the diaper bag and found one of Mateo's teething biscuits.

"Why's she tied up?" Sophie demanded. "Where's her mother?"

"Hush!" Gladys put a finger to her lips.

The fence was the same height as she was. When she hooked the toe of her sneaker in a link, the dog turned, beautiful eyes shining.

You.

True Blue.

The house's curtains stayed shut as Gladys climbed the fence.

"Your bowls are empty. Are you hungry?" She held out the teething biscuit. "You are, aren't you?"

Did the woman leave her outside all the time? Being homeless would be terrible, but having a home and being shut out of it? That was even worse. Gladys kept softly calling, gently coaxing, leaning over the fence. Her arm began to prickle from holding out the biscuit, and the fence's top rail dug into her ribs, but she didn't give up. She *couldn't* give up. Of all the places she might have gone for a walk, she'd come here. Something had led her to True. There was a bond between them, something powerful and meant to be.

Wriggle wriggle—the dog inched out. Her sweet face, with its fur like a spill of milk. Her middle, her hind paws, and finally her funny, crooked tail. She took a few steps, then thought better of it. By now Gladys's arm was numb but she held it steady, determined not to scare True, who needed to know someone cared about her. Not everyone in the world was as heartless as her owner.

"It's not your fault," she whispered. "You deserve to be loved."

She felt that space open inside her, dark and echoey as a cave. A chill went through her, but she held firm, because even as the hollow inside gaped wider, True edged closer. The wash line went taut till at last she couldn't come any nearer. Digging the tips of her shoes into the fence and gripping the railing with her free hand, Gladys stretched herself as far as she possibly could, and then maybe a little farther. Now True stretched, too. Her cold, wet nose grazed Gladys's fingers.

Lifting her head, she took the biscuit as delicately as a princess at a tea party.

Gladys was so happy, she lost her grip on the fence and tumbled forward. Her hands scrabbled for the fence but came up empty and now she was falling, falling . . .

"Gladys!" Sophie screeched.

She lay on the needly ground, and where the dark space had been, she now had a terrible, chest-burning pain. She rolled over to find True looming above her, mouth open, tongue lolling. The jaws of a furry crocodile! Her breath was meaty and her gums were spotted and her teeth were not teeth at all but fangs. Breaking out in goosebumps, Gladys understood, this was *an animal.*

"Are you dead?" Sophie cried.

The front door flew open and the woman charged across the yard.

"Good God!" She kicked an empty dish out of her way. Now she loomed over Gladys, too. "You? You again!"

"The witch!" Sophie stumbled backward into the stroller, which woke Mateo, who commenced screaming as if someone had dropped a snake on his head.

"You little demon!" The woman yanked Gladys to her feet. "Now you're teasing a dog?"

"I wasn't. I'd never!"

The woman's face was splotchy. Strands of hair stuck to her cheeks. She'd been crying, Gladys realized, though what could make someone like her cry?

"Don't lie to me." Her fingers dug into Gladys's arm. "I saw you with my own eyes."

"You're not nice to her!" Gladys said. "Why do you even have her?"

"Mind your own business, you brat!" Her eyelashes stuck together in spiky clumps. Her breath was sour with cigarettes.

"Let her go, witch!" Sophie rattled the fence. "There's no such thing as you! Go away!"

Mateo's wailing reached fever pitch. True Blue had something dark green in her mouth, Gladys's hat! It must have fallen off when she tumbled. True dropped it and began to bark.

"Pookie! Shut your trap!" Letting go of Gladys, the woman lunged toward the dog who yelped and dove back inside her house.

"We don't say *shut your trap*!" Sophie said.

"You think I'm a witch?" The woman spun around. "You're right. Bother me or that dog again and I'll boil you in my pot! No. I'll eat you raw!"

Gladys scrambled over the fence, grabbed Sophie, set her in the stroller, and shoved it down the sidewalk with strength she didn't know she had. But when she looked back, she saw True Blue had come out of her doghouse and gotten helplessly tangled in her rope. The woman ignored her. She stood beneath the tree, trying to light a cigarette, flicking her lighter again and again with shaking hands.

Mateo wailed as if his tiny heart was breaking. It *was* heartbreaking. It was infuriating. *That* dog, the woman said. Not *my*. A person who loved her dog would never talk that way. Plus—Pookie? What a humiliating name. Once when Gladys had complained to her mother about her own archaic name, Mama replied, "'A rose by any other name would still smell as sweet.'" What people called a rose made no difference to the rose, so this was a false comparison. Gladys despised lazy thinking!

"I want my mother," Sophie said in a tiny voice. "I want Mommy."

Out of breath, Gladys stopped at the corner. She should go back. She'd let True down. She'd made things even worse, because True had trusted her, at least for a moment, only to be disappointed and abandoned by yet another human.

"I want Mommy." Tears rolled down Sophie's cheeks, and Gladys wiped them with the hem of her shirt.

"It's okay." She smoothed Sophie's hair. As she fastened the stroller straps, she said, "It'll be okay." This was what you promised sprouts, whether you believed it or not.

When Gladys began to push the stroller again, Mateo quieted. Babies and dogs—they had no words. They depended on you to figure out what they needed, then to help them get it. Gladys bent her weight to the stroller. She was angry, but some other feeling was slipping around inside her, too. She tried to name it—what was it? Her phone dinged with a text.

You are the best of the best of the best, wrote Mama, followed by a zillion hearts. *Hurry home—cold lemonade waiting.*

Mama! She insisted every bad contained good and if you looked, you'd find it. Though Gladys could not think of one single, solitary good thing about True's owner, she could still see her face, shiny with sorrow. Why was she crying? Was it possible that somehow, somewhere inside her, a heart was still trying to beat?

Who knew why Jude's stricken face rose in her mind now?

It would be a long walk to his house with a stroller the size of a small boat. And it wasn't as if Jude had shown any sign of wanting to see her again in this lifetime or the next. Yet how could she turn her back on True? She needed to do something, though she wasn't sure what, and maybe Jude would have an idea. Maybe he'd want to help. Or maybe he wouldn't want to, but she could persuade him to. Gladys had great faith in her own powers of persuasion.

She re-wound her scarf, put her head down, and pushed.

Jude

Home from that messed-up walk, Jude tried the summer reading book. The first few pages hooked you in, but then it cut to boring, slo-mo stuff, leaving you hanging. Jude really hated when books tricked you like that.

Maybe some math. He was better at math than reading any day. He got his school tablet, but Spider wanted him to play Chucky and when Spider wanted something, forget it. Jude had to hold his little brother on his lap and say how cute he was, then act scared out of his mind when Spider started doing an evil laugh.

With Spider, if something was fun once, it was fun twelve million times. Jude was pretending to run for his life again when he got a whiff of something gross. Looking out the window, he saw old Mr. Peters spraying his grass.

Jude slammed the side window shut. Went to the front window and what the—?

That girl! Pushing two kids in a massive stroller. She was stronger than she looked, that was for sure.

Jude ducked back.

Peeked again.

She jabbed the doorbell. That doorbell hadn't worked in years.

It was kind of scary, how determined she looked.

Also kind of cool.

She jabbed the doorbell again. Then started knocking.

This could be trouble, said his brain.

Open the door, said whatever the opposite of a brain was.

Gladys

Gladys rang Jude's doorbell and when nobody answered, she rang it again. Meanwhile, her phone pinged with another text from Mama, this one asking where she was so long.

Mateo is blissfully asleep, Gladys texted back. *Sophie is enjoying the walk.* She added a string of smiling, winking, kiss-blowing emojis.

"It stinks here," Sophie said, pinching her nose.

Time to head home, Mama texted.

"I don't like that thing." Sophie pointed at the mutilated fir tree.

Gladys tried knocking. Across the driveway, the neat-as-a-pin neighbor was spraying something with a highly unpleasant odor. *Noxious*, thought Gladys—such a perfect word. She raised her fist to knock again just as the door opened.

Jude smiled. The sun finding a minuscule crack in a wall of storm clouds—that's what kind of smile it was. It was entirely possible Jude didn't even know he'd smiled.

But Gladys did. Gladys saw.

A foot taller than she was, he peered down at the top of her head.

"Why's your hair full of pine needles?"

"What?" She ran a hand through it, scattering needles like a dried-up Christmas tree. She thought fleetingly of her lost green velvet hat. "Her house. There's a tall tree out front and—"

"Whose house?"

Spider hurtled out the door. He wore a Chucky mask, but that wasn't the most remarkable thing about him.

"He's naked!" Sophie shrieked with such delight she startled Mateo awake again. His eyes went wide. His arms flew out. He opened his mouth and sucked breath forever until . . .

"Whoa!" Jude clapped his hands over his ears.

"Siren," said Gladys, picking the baby up. "Mateo is a siren that's assumed the form of a human." She jiggled him on her hip as Spider, a bandage on his forehead, took the baby's place beside Sophie in the stroller. Fortunately, he wasn't 100 percent naked. He wore Thomas the Tank Engine underpants.

"Get your butt out of that stroller," Jude said.

"You said *butt*!" crowed Sophie, who'd abruptly changed her mind about how much she hated it here. "I pooped in the bushes," she told Spider.

"I pooped on Jude's head," Spider said, sending Sophie into a giggle rhapsody. He offered her his Chucky mask, which Sophie accepted with delight.

"I guess Spider survived," Gladys said.

"Yeah. Too bad."

Gladys's phone pinged with another text from her mother, but she ignored it.

"Whose house?" Jude asked again. His yellow hair hung over his eyes and when he pushed it back, she felt as if he was pushing her away, too. Then she reminded herself he'd smiled when he saw her. Against his will maybe, but still. She switched the wailing Mateo to her other hip and jiggled him harder.

"The woman with the dog."

"For real?" He took the baby, held him close, and rubbed a circle on his little back. Mateo drew a shuddery breath and rested his head on Jude's chest. "Where does she live?"

"Wait. How'd you do that?" Gladys asked.

"What?"

"The only one who can ever soothe Mateo is my mother."

Jude shrugged. "Spider gave me lots of practice. Anyway where does she live? Under a rock, right?"

"On Seventh Street. Mrs. Marsh lives there—did you have her for third grade? She didn't have any food or water, the dog I mean, so I gave her a biscuit but I fell over the fence, which is how I got needles in my hair, I guess. She, the lady I mean, came out and hurled all kinds of threats at me, plus it turns out True Blue's really named Pookie, and—"

"I thought its name was Spooky. Where'd you get True Blue?"

Gladys ducked her head. She hadn't meant to tell him *that*. "That's what I call her. True for short."

"You mean *him*." Was he about to smile again?

"I checked. She's definitely a girl."

Jude's cheeks pinked up. Gladys resisted thinking how cute that made him look. She didn't want to get sidetracked.

"I've never really liked dogs, to tell you the truth," she said. "But True's different."

Should she tell him about their wordless communication? How powerful forces had drawn her to True? How she was sure the dog was looking for something she'd lost? Mateo bunched a fold of Jude's T-shirt in his little fist. Babies didn't trust just anyone, Mama always said. Babies *knew*.

"You can tell by her sensitive, intelligent eyes. You know the way she sits still, gazing into the distance? Like she's waiting for something?"

Gladys wanted to add, *Waiting to be truly loved*, but was too embarrassed. The way Jude looked at her, though, made her hope he understood. He glanced away, looked back, then suddenly screwed up his face.

"Your imagination's out of control," he said. "That dog's eyes are weird. No way you can tell what it's thinking." He shook his head. "You're really lucky it didn't bite you."

"You're wrong. She needs help. I—"

A car turned into the driveway and a pretty woman got out. She looked totally harmless, even nice, but Spider jumped out of the stroller and Jude got a panicked look.

"You gotta bounce," he told Gladys, handing back the sleeping Mateo.

The woman had to be his mother. She had identical blond hair and deep brown eyes. Her work uniform was rumpled and she walked as if her feet hurt, but she regarded Gladys in a not-unfriendly way.

"That baby's half as big as you." She smiled and touched the bottom of Mateo's foot. The scar on her upper lip turned the smile crooked and made her look . . . Gladys searched for the word. *Fragile? Breakable?* His mother tapped Jude's chest. "I hope you told your friend you're under house arrest."

"We were just leaving," Gladys said. Jude had lulled Mateo into a sleep so deep, the baby didn't even stir when she set him back in the stroller. She took the Chucky mask from Sophie and handed it to Spider. "Very nice to meet you."

As she heaved the stroller down the front walk, she heard Jude's mother ask him, "What in the name of God is that stink?"

"Mr. Peters."

"It smells like a freaking skunk convention! And who's that cute little girl?"

"I don't know," he said.

"Gladys." She spun around. "My name is *Gladys*."

Jude

Gladys! A name for somebody who made doilies and took her teeth out at night.

But the way she said it—shouted it practically—you could tell she loved her name. She loved her whole life, anybody could see it. She was so...

He didn't know the word. *Confident*, maybe. *Sure of herself.* Look how she dressed! What was that scarf about? She didn't care what people thought. She was the size of a third grader but she talked like she was in high school.

All that stuff she said about the dog? Like he felt the same way. Like he agreed it was some really special dog.

True.

Jude shook his head.

He couldn't believe the dog didn't even have water.

• • •

That night, Mom kept teasing him about the big-eyed girl crushing on him.

"I don't even know her!"

"I saw the way she looked at you, mister."

Jude made a puke noise.

"Just remember," Mom said. "You're grounded. I catch you making a jailbreak and..."

"Mom! No way I care about that girl!"

His mother laughed. It was her real laugh, the one that reminded Jude of how a breeze can blow through a tree so the leaves lift and show their softer, secret side.

"Keep protesting, mister. Go on!"

She messed up his hair, said he'd done a good job getting the paint stuff. Tomorrow he could start preparing the walls. She wanted to get a new shower curtain and bath mat. Maybe some towels, if she could find nice ones on sale. She walked around humming, smoothing out the doilies.

When Mom was happy like this, all Jude wanted was to make it last. Last and last.

Gladys

She couldn't believe he didn't even remember her name.

Back home, Sophie wouldn't stop talking about the underwear boy.

"Is this a new imaginary friend?" Mama asked.

"You know how Sophie is!" Gladys shrugged.

"You were gone a long time. And you didn't answer my last texts."

"I never poop in the bushes," Sophie announced, sending Mama's eyebrows skyward.

"I'm a little confused here," Mama said.

"Well, I'm a little overheated and exhausted," Gladys said.

She went to the sink to wash her hands and splash water on her face, providing a visual aid to how she was too worn out to talk. She didn't dare look at her mother, afraid she'd blurt out everything. Mama would say it was sad about True, but she'd also be shocked Gladys had been to the house of a stranger at all, let alone one she knew had anger issues, let alone with the sprouts, not to mention tried to pet an unknown dog, not to mention going to Jude's house, all without permission. Mama would re-state her rules and reasons, then hug Gladys and say she knew she meant well but good intentions didn't always result in good outcomes, did Gladys understand that? And then she'd assume the matter was settled.

Mama never got really angry. She was more about explaining. So it wasn't fear of getting in trouble that kept Gladys at the sink, washing her hands even though they were by now perfectly clean. If Mama knew, she'd make Gladys promise never to go back to that house. And Gladys couldn't.

She wouldn't.

When at last she shut off the water and turned around, her mother was thoughtfully pushing her lower lip with one nail-bitten finger.

"It's been a tough few days, sugar." Her smile was tired but gentle. "How about that cold lemonade?"

That sounded so good.

"No thank you," Gladys said.

A crack appeared in the kitchen floor. Not a real one, though it might as well have been. The crack zigzagged from one wall to the other, as if their house was having its own personal earthquake. Gladys and Mama were stranded on opposite sides, both unhappy.

Sophie was the one who broke the silence.

"There's no such thing as witches," she whispered.

Jude

The next morning, Mom hoisted her massive purse onto her shoulder. Tapped the to-do list taped to the fridge.

"Above all," she said, "make sure—"

"—Spider stays out of trouble. Got it, Mom."

She gave him that look, then shook her head. Touched the tip of his nose.

Two seconds after she was gone, Spider started up. He wanted to go play with Soapie.

"Sophie!" Jude said. "And no way."

"We can sneak. I won't tell."

"Yeah right. Anyway, I don't know where she lives." Jude was lying. He remembered Gladys's address. Don't ask him why.

"I know where."

"No you don't."

"I can find them."

Jude set Spider on the couch and switched on *Thomas*. He was going to paint the bathroom like no bathroom in the history of bathrooms ever got painted. When he was done and Mom saw his professional-level job, she was going to faint. She was going to say, *This is what I'm talking about, mister. Stand back 'cause I'm about to bust with pride.*

Nothing could stop him.

He lugged a kitchen chair into the bathroom, put in his ear-buds. Grabbed his weapon: the Scraper. Paint chips flew around like a pink blizzard. He yawned and one landed in his mouth. He leaned sideways, one hand on the shower curtain bar, got up in the far corner.

He made grilled cheese for lunch, and it turned out killer. This day was going all right. Later he'd give that stupid summer reading book another try.

He got his school tablet. Clicked on a game his brother could do. For an extra bribe, a bag of Cheetos.

"Be good, okay? I gotta work on the bathroom some more. Then I'll play with you."

"Play with me now."

"Just a little longer."

Back to work. The job was satisfying in a gross way, like picking a scab. He turned up his music.

After a while he pulled out his earbuds and took a break to use the bathroom for what it was meant for, then washed his face. Picked up the scraper, suddenly noticed how quiet the house was.

Uh-oh.

Kitchen—empty. Tablet covered with cheesy-orange fingerprints—on the floor.

"Spider?" Not in the living room. Not in either bedroom. "Spider-Man!"

He tore out into the backyard. He looked behind the trash cans, but he already knew. His brother was gone. He'd taken off.

Jude kicked over a lawn chair. Back inside, he grabbed the house keys and locked up. Out front, Mr. Peters was watering his flowers.

"You see Spider?" Jude called.

Mr. Peters pointed toward the corner. "He said something about soap."

"Thanks." Jude took off running. He'd gone a full block before he realized he still held the scraper.

Gladys

Sitting on the front steps, taking a much-needed afternoon break, Gladys phoned Chickie. Annabelle picked up.

"Hold on a minute," she said.

Chickie wasn't allowed to have a cell phone yet, so Gladys had to wait while Annabelle hunted her down. Cobwebs were practically growing over her before Chickie came on.

"What's up?" Her best friend sounded suspiciously cheerful, as if nothing was wrong. As if she hadn't betrayed Gladys with someone named Morgan. Gladys had planned to bring this up and patiently listen to Chickie's apologies, but hearing her friend's voice made her realize just how lonesome she was.

"A lot actually," she began, but paused. Was that whispering in the background? Was someone else there? "Anyway," she went on, speaking more quickly, "just so you know. I don't hold a grudge about you ditching me. I'm prepared to be magnanimous about it."

A giggle.

"Chickie? Is something funny?"

"Why do you talk to me like that?"

"What?" Gladys sat up straighter. "Like what?"

"Like you're a teacher and I'm the kid who needs special help."

"I don't!" Gladys was flabbergasted. "I love talking to you. You always listen to me."

"And listen and listen and listen." Chickie blew a breath. "That's all I ever get to do, because you never stop talking."

Gladys was sure she heard more whispering in the background. Was it that Morgan? Gladys swallowed.

"You never told me this before," she said.

"Well. I guess I am now."

"Okay. I mean, not okay. We can talk. I mean, you can talk." Gladys watched a big ant crawl across her foot like she was a rock or clod of dirt. "Anyway, the reason I called is because we really need to plan our traditional back-to-school shopping trip."

"I don't know. I might not have time."

"What?"

"I know what'll happen. We'll go to the Goodwill and Aunt Annie's Attic and you'll talk about how cool all the old clothes are, then we'll go to Target and you'll say how boring and generic everything is." Chickie blew another breath. "Well, I happen to like Target!"

"Okay. You can like Target."

"You say that, but you don't mean it."

"Well, Target is kind of generic and—"

"See? You don't value my opinions."

"I can't believe you said that."

"See what I mean?"

"Why are you acting this way? Someone must be poisoning your mind."

Whispering.

"I'm sorry, Gladys." For a second Gladys believed her, but then Chickie added, "I guess I'll see you in school." She hung up.

Years ago, Gladys had accidentally stepped onto a yellow-jacket nest. They'd swarmed up from under the ground, surrounding her, attacking from all sides. At first she couldn't even tell what was happening. It felt as if the air itself had turned against her, shooting her with invisible fiery arrows.

That was a good description of how she felt now.

Sophie slipped out the front door, wearing a pipe-cleaner crown. When she sat down and leaned into Gladys, she was warm and solid and, to tell the truth, not completely unwelcome. At this moment in time, Sophie might be the only friend Gladys possessed.

What had happened? She'd have sworn on her half-a-million-word dictionary that she and Chickie were best friends, but she'd been wrong. So wrong. Chickie preferred a girl who liked Target and probably had a two-syllable vocabulary.

"It's okay," whispered Sophie. "Let the sad out."

When Gladys looked at herself in the mirror, she saw one person, but when Chickie looked at Gladys, she must see someone else. Not the person Gladys thought she was, but someone . . . unlikable. Bossy and self-centered. Two totally different definitions of *Gladys*.

Which one was right? They couldn't both be, that was for sure.

All summer, Gladys had been counting on a friend who wasn't really there. What if there was nothing in this world you could really, fully depend on? What if everyone was walking around with their own separate, secret versions of life? What if even the people you counted on most could change their minds about you?

Could abandon you?

What if it was your own fault?

"You're the best babysitter in the uniworse." Sophie patted Gladys's knee. "After Ms. Suza."

What if no matter how hard you tried to understand the universe, to pin it down and name it, nothing was for sure?

Sophie un-Velcroed herself from Gladys. "You got clothes on," she said, disappointed.

Gladys lifted her head. Blinking tears, she saw Jude and his little brother coming toward them.

Jude

Yo." Jude tried to sound all casual, like he hadn't seen her crying.

She slid the back of her hand across her eyes. Sat up straight. Good! He liked it much better when she was cheery and annoying. Sophie hugged Spider like they were long-lost cousins.

"Aren't you grounded?" Gladys asked.

She was wearing shoes that belonged in a grandma's closet and a bracelet with jangly things. Somebody needed to tell her she was too old to play dress-up.

"Prison break," he said.

She was so little. He remembered that fable about the mouse saving the lion and the lion returning the favor. He really needed to sit down. His legs were rubber bands.

"Could you please sit down?" she said. "I'm getting a neck ache looking up at you."

He sat on the step below her. Sophie and Spider poked in the dirt.

"Can I ask you something?" she said then.

He hated when people said that. It usually meant they had something they wanted to tell you, not ask you. Some lesson they were about to lay on you. *Can I ask—why do you make so many bad choices?*

But this girl—no predicting. She leaned forward. Her hair, the only big thing about her, grazed his cheek. He got a whiff of coconut.

"Do I talk too much?"

"Umm. Yeah."

She sat back. For a second he was scared she'd start crying again, but instead she busted out a smile.

"At least you tell the truth." She sniffed. "Unlike some people."

Now she'd hog up the conversation. Fine with him, because no way he felt like explaining why he was here. He didn't want to tell how his brother had run away, and he'd lost his mind looking for him, hearing the train whistle, picturing Spider darting out, the train sucking him under, how he was practically crying by the time he actually found Spy outside Freddy's Bar and Grill. How his brother had his arms inside his too-big basketball jersey so he was a little sniveling cocoon.

Jude would never tell Gladys—never tell anybody—what his brother said then.

When a person does something stupid, you don't reward them. When your brother runs away to find a friend he calls Soapie, you punish him. The last thing you do is take him straight to her house like he wants.

Yeah.

Sophie and Spider were on all fours, scooping dirt and barking like little dogs with juicy bones.

"Quit that!" Jude ordered. Waste of breath.

Inside the house, a baby cried. Gladys jumped up.

"Let's go where we can talk in private," she said.

She led them around the side of the house. Looking over a

white fence he saw a backyard packed with toys. A nice syca-more, too.

"I'm glad you came," she said. "Even though, to be honest, I'm pretty surprised."

"It was Spider." His brother was trying to scale the fence as Sophie watched admiringly. Jude plucked him off. "All his idea."

"Oh. Okay."

She dug a knuckle into first one eye, then the other. Maybe he had her wrong? Maybe she wasn't so 100 percent happy as he thought?

"My so-called best friend just informed me she's sick of me," she said.

"That bites." He could tell her about Jabari. Same, he could say. But then he'd have to explain about the fortress and how bad he'd messed up. "Who needs them anyway, right?"

Out of nowhere, she said, "When I came to your house yes-terday? I was hoping you'd help me with True."

Spider was back on the fence. You'd swear he had sticky pads, like a tree frog. Jude pulled him off and set him down.

"What if we could go see her without getting caught?" she said. "To reassure her. Give her some love. Some hope."

"Hope of what?"

She bit her lip. A train whistled in the distance.

"That lady is evil," he said. "But it's not like you can kidnap her dog."

"I didn't say that."

"If you show up then leave, how's that going to help? You'd just make Pookie feel worse."

"Don't call her that humiliating name." She sniffed again, then gave a slow nod. "You're right. We'd only be giving her false hope."

Jude had never heard those two words put together before. Hope was supposed to be a good thing, not something that hurt you. But as soon as she said it, he knew what she was talking about. Right then, for one second, he imagined telling her what Spider said when Jude found him all alone, hunched up and crying.

I can't find my friend, he'd said, burying his face against Jude. And then, *Where's my daddy?*

He couldn't tell Gladys that.

He wouldn't tell her that.

Still. He wanted to tell her something.

"So, my brother had a meltdown. I tried all the stuff that usually calms him, but the only thing that worked was saying we'd come here."

"That's so sweet." Her face lit up and all of a sudden, he saw how some people might call her pretty.

"He wanted to see Soapie," he said, and that made her laugh.

A nice laugh.

Spider tried the fence again. Jude pulled him off again. His little brother was filthy from digging with Sophie. A walking dirt bomb. Great. *Great*. Jude would have to give him a bath. Then he'd have to clean the tub. He was already behind schedule on the paint job.

"We gotta go. If my mom gets home and finds us gone..." He clutched his throat and bugged his eyes. She turned up her smile. What did she not understand about being dead?

"It's not your fault he ran away," she said. "And when he needed comfort, you found it for him. Once you explain to her—"

"That's not how it works in my house, okay?"

"But your mother's so nice."

What was she even talking about? *Who* was she talking about?

"She's so pretty and her smile is luminous. You two look so much alike."

Did she actually sound...jealous? That couldn't be.

The back door opened and some little kids tumbled out. Then a big woman with a long red braid, carrying the human siren and a bowl of crackers. Seeing them on the other side of the fence, she looked surprised.

"Gladys? Have we got company?"

Gladys introduced them, though Jude could tell she didn't want to. What was that about?

"Why are you standing out there?" Her mother had the exact same smile as Gladys. "Come on in the backyard and have a snack."

"Snack!" Spider grabbed Jude's hand. "Pleeeeeeease?"

Gladys

In the backyard, where the sprouts were zigzagging around, Mama conducted a quick but thorough interrogation. How did Gladys and Jude know each other? Ah, school! What grade was he in? Where did they live? Wow, Spider was a strong boy to walk all the way here!

Standing under the tree, shifting from foot to foot, Jude let Gladys do all the talking. He pulled what looked like a paint scraper out of the pocket where he usually kept a book, studied it, and put it back. When Mama offered him the bowl of Goldfish crackers, he stuffed a handful into his mouth.

"Maybe I didn't explain," Gladys said, steering him away from her inquisitive mother. "We run a home daycare."

"So . . ." He swallowed the crackers. "So Sophie and the human siren aren't related to you?"

"What a terrifying thought!"

Lily, toddling past, tripped and face-planted on Jude's big shoe. Before she could even think about crying, Jude scooped her up, airplaned her over his head, set her back down, and gave her a fist bump. Lily stared up at him in wonder, then hugged his leg. Jude gave a grunt. Or maybe it was a laugh. Gladys was almost getting used to his nonverbal tendencies. She could tell he loved his brother, and she was convinced he cared about True. He just didn't know how to say it. Or maybe he just didn't *want* to say it. Maybe he didn't see any *need* to say it. He was like a tree. The underground part, the roots and rootlets you couldn't see, grew as wide and deep as the aboveground part grew tall.

Mama was blowing bubbles for the sprouts to chase. *Pop!* the babies said. *Pop!* When one landed in Jude's curls, Gladys noticed bits of what might be pink paint. Just as she was considering plucking one of the rosy slivers, he cupped his hands around his mouth.

"Time's up, Spy," he megaphoned. "We gotta go!"

His brother completely ignored him, standard sprout behavior. Gladys leaned closer, lowering her voice.

"I know you're grounded and everything, but can't you stay a little longer? We didn't finish talking about you-know-what. I'm thinking that if we put our heads together . . ."

"Spy! You heard me!"

"Excuse me," Gladys said. "I thought I was talking."

"I'm counting to three!" Jude said. "One. Two."

Like he'd heard a starter pistol, Spider took off running.

Jude

It wasn't a big yard and Spider did two laps easy. Dodged the sandbox, hurdled a big wheel. The third time he went by, Jude nabbed him, but Spider wriggled free.

When he was only two, Spider made it up onto Auntie Jewel's garage roof. He'd climbed bookshelves in the library and displays in the grocery store. Scaffolding on buildings and who knew how many ladders, fences, and trees. A swing set was nothing. Just like that, he straddled the top. It was the old-fashioned metal kind, a little rickety. Sophie and the other kids gathered around and craned their necks like they were at the circus.

"Get down," Jude commanded.

"I can't."

"You got up, you can get down."

"I'm too scared!" Spider made big, helpless eyes. A look guaranteed to melt the heart of anyone who didn't know him. But Jude knew him.

"Don't play with me! Get. Down. Now."

The little kids went quiet. They looked at Jude like he was some kind of bad guy. He felt his face go red.

"You heard me!" He smacked Spider's leg.

"Don't!" Sophie cried. "No hitting!"

"Jude," Ms. Suza said. "I don't think—"

"I can handle this." Jude's voice came out louder than he meant it to. "He's my brother. I know how to handle my own brother."

The siren baby started crying. Like they'd heard a secret signal, a bunch of other kids did, too. Jude was so embarrassed he wanted to spit.

"Get down!" He shook his fist at Spider.

"Jude." Ms. Suza's face was round and wide, with wrinkles, freckles, a space between her front teeth you could slot a quarter through. Even though it had all those distractions going on, the main thing about her face was it was calm. Calm like the moon.

The sycamore arched over their heads. Old bark crumbling, creamy new bark peeking out, like the tree was making some kind of promise. When Ms. Suza's hand came to rest on his shoulder, a hush went through him. *Safe*, he thought. This place is safe. Another kind of fortress, one with toys and snacks.

But they had to go. They didn't belong here. Jude shrugged off Ms. Suza and smacked his brother's foot.

"Let's not threaten him, okay?" Ms. Suza said. "The best thing to do when someone is scared—"

"He's not scared. He's hardheaded."

"I see that. But he's also only what? Three or so?"

"He's four."

Ms. Suza's brow puckered. Something new started going on in her eyes. A knowing. Like, *I know what's right, and I'm trying to show you.* She thought she was helping, but really? Really she was showing him what was wrong with him. Like a counselor telling him he could do anything if he tried hard enough. Bullying, that's what it was. For all her soft ways, Ms. Suza was a bully.

95

Maybe this was how Mom felt when Auntie Jewel gave her advice.

Maybe he was like Mom.

"Spider, honey, don't be scared," Ms. Suza said. "You're not in trouble. We just don't want you to get hurt. Can you scoot one leg over very, very slowly?" She handed Gladys the siren baby, then held up her arms. "That's right."

Back off! Jude wanted to say. *He's my brother!* But Spider was under her moon-face spell.

"There you go." Ms. Suza smiled encouragingly. "That's it. That's my boy. That's my buddy."

Spider was in her arms. She brushed some dirt off his forehead and touched the grubby bandage. Jude could feel Gladys watching him, but no way he'd look back at her. She'd be wearing the same look as her mother. *Poor you.*

"Sorry for the trouble," he said. "We're going now."

"I'll just take him inside and wash him up," Ms. Suza said.

"It's okay. We're good."

"It'll only take a minute."

"We got water at our house, too. We got soap and water and everything we need, just so you know."

He heard Gladys suck a breath. Ms. Suza's eyes clouded over, and the strange thing was, she looked sorry. Like she didn't mean to be a bully. Like really, all she wanted was to help him, and she was sorry if she went about it the wrong way.

"Okay." Ms. Suza gently set Spider on his feet. "But I hope you two will come back. We'd love to have you again."

How could she say that, after seeing how much trouble Spider caused? Jude glanced around one more time. This place was another planet. Guess who was the alien? He grabbed his brother's hand, headed for the gate.

"Anytime," Ms. Suza called. "Goodbye, Spider! Goodbye, buddy!"

"Bye bye!" Sophie blew kisses. "Bye bye, BFF!"

Gladys came tripping after him in her grandma shoes.

"That was rude! Why were you so rude to my mother?"

Jude swung his brother up on his shoulders and kept going.

"I asked you a question!" she said.

"I wasn't being rude. I was sticking up for myself."

"That makes no sense."

"Oh yeah? Guess what? Big news. You don't know everything."

She stopped. "I never said I—"

"Your mother's like...like a fairy godmother or something. That's cool. Good for you! But don't think that makes you better than me. In case you didn't notice, nobody's calling *you* normal."

The look on her face almost made him take it back. Instead, he made it worse.

"And that dog? Forget it. There's nothing you can do about it."

"But—"

"Or maybe you can, what do I know. Just leave me out of that mess. I don't have time for it. You're so freaking smart, figure it out yourself."

You'd think she'd yell something after him. This girl who never ran out of words.

But as he walked away, all he heard was his own stupid feet slapping the sidewalk.

Gladys

Spider's small for his age," Mama said that night at dinner. "And the way he climbed the swing set was so reckless. He could have gotten a concussion or broken bone. No wonder he has stitches! I'm worried about him."

Gladys picked up a chicken nugget shaped like the letter *A*, then set it back down. Mama hadn't cooked a real dinner since Angela quit. They ate the same food she served the sprouts: chicken nuggets, carrot sticks, applesauce. No knives required.

"I hope he doesn't have lead poisoning. Way too many houses around here still have lead paint," Mama continued. "The landlords are responsible, but unless the town gets after them, nothing happens. And this town . . ."

Dada had specks of chicken coating caught in his humiliating beard. Today at Crooked River, they'd had him substitute in the candle-making building, and he wore Band-Aids on the backs of both hands. Melted wax was hot.

After a full day of taking care of other people's children, most humans would want to talk about anything else. Not Mama. On and on she went about lead poisoning causing hyperactivity and poor impulse control. Gladys picked up an *L*-shaped nugget and set it next to the *A*.

"Gladys?" Mama paused. "You're very quiet tonight."

Within a few hours, two people, one Gladys thought was her best friend and one she hoped was *becoming* her friend, had both told her in no uncertain terms to get out of their lives.

Gladys was a total reject.

This was not something she'd ever felt before.

Though she must have! She must have felt it when her mother gave her up to foster care. Even tiny babies knew who their true mother was. Gladys saw this every day when parents came to pick up their children. Even Mateo, who adored Mama, basically leaped out of her arms when he saw his mother. When Gladys's birth mother gave her up, Gladys must have known. Even her tiny, wordless brain must have understood—she was among strangers now.

Had she thought her mother would come back for her? When arms reached down to her, did she look up, hoping to see her real mother's face?

"Sugar?"

Mama came around the table. She circled Gladys's shoulders with her arms and rested her chin on Gladys's head.

Gladys stared at her plate where she'd spelled out *ALON* in chicken nuggets. She couldn't find an *E*.

"I know someone who needs a hug," Mama said.

But Gladys didn't need a hug. She tried to think of the word for what she needed but couldn't.

This was another first.

She pushed back her chair, startling Mama, who stepped away with an *oof.*

"I hate chicken nuggets," she said.

Mama looked baffled. "No you don't," she said.

"Guess what? Big news! You don't know everything! Especially about me!"

She charged out of the room. She heard her mother start to follow, and then her father's quiet voice.

"Let her go," he said.

"But . . ."

"She's growing up, Suzanna. This was bound to happen."

What? What was bound to happen?

Jude

Next day—no paint scraper. It must've fallen out of his pocket when he was chasing Spider around Gladys's yard. Jude thought about going back to get it but decided he couldn't risk violating house arrest again.

There was another thing he couldn't risk. He didn't know the word for it, though.

Gladys would. She'd slap a word on how he felt. She'd name the thing he couldn't risk. And then she'd start talking about the dog again.

He tried scraping the bathroom walls with a spatula.

He'd be graduated from high school before he was done.

When he threw the spatula against the wall, it bounced off and hit his bare foot.

"Aargh!"

His outraged face loomed up in the mirror. Jude did a double take.

Gladys was right. He did look like his mother.

Jude told Spider he'd be right back. Mr. Peters opened his door before Jude could even knock.

"Hello, neighbor." His voice made you think of God, if God had a comb-over and wore bedroom slippers. "How nice to see you!"

"Mr. Peters, do you by any chance have a paint scraper I could borrow?"

"Of course! Come in!"

Jude waited in the living room. A couch, a coffee table, a painting of a sunset. Twin armchairs in front of the TV. Everything clean as a whistle. Whatever that meant.

"Here you go." Mr. Peters came back with two scrapers. "Are you painting?"

"Yeah. Our bathroom."

"The key to a good paint job is to prepare the surface well. Be careful with these. They're sharp." He handed them over. "Is there anything else you need? Brushes? Drop cloths?"

"This'll do it. Thanks a lot."

"Anytime, Jude. Anytime at all. Keep them as long as you need."

These scrapers were deluxe. Way better than the cheap one he'd had. He was going to tear up that bathroom!

Gladys

Jude's paint scraper was in her sock drawer, where she'd put it after she found it in the grass. She'd considered returning it, but he didn't deserve the favor. If he really wanted the scraper, let him come get it himself. And if he did, she knew exactly what she'd say.

My mother and I were only trying to help you. I'm willing to forgive your rudeness. He'd pull that sullen face and she'd say, *All right, you don't have to apologize. I can be magnanimous about this.*

Maybe she shouldn't say *magnanimous.* Considering how Chickie had reacted to it.

Generous. Maybe she could say she was willing to be generous? Even though she really, truly meant *magnanimous,* a much nobler word.

Why was she even thinking about this? It was hopeless. He was hopeless. A human fortress, that was Jude.

Every Saturday, she and Mama cleaned the house. As they vacuumed up Cheerios, scrubbed sticky furniture, and polished finger-and-nose-printed windows, Mama sang along with her old-timey favorites: "Here Comes the Sun," "What a Wonderful World," "Feelin' Groovy". Gladys knew Mama was hoping she'd join in. But today, happy songs seemed as fake as diet soda with its carcinogenic artificial sweetener.

103

Their Saturday routine was, once they finished cleaning, they kicked back and rewarded themselves with a movie. Mama made her famous cheese popcorn and they swigged pop from tall glasses without worrying someone would knock them over.

Today though, Gladys said she had someplace to go. Disappointment flitted across Mama's face.

"To Chickie's?"

"No."

"Jude's?"

"After how rude he was to you?"

Mama pulled the bandanna off her hair and used it to rub a spot they'd missed on the coffee table.

"It's plain as the space between my teeth, that boy could use a friend. I'm guessing he and Spider have different fathers, don't they?"

Gladys had never thought about that, though as soon as Mama said it, it seemed blatantly obvious. Which was annoying.

"Jude doesn't discuss personal matters," she said.

"Boys can be like that." Mama smiled. "I dated your dada for six months before I found out he liked to bake. He was afraid I'd think he was a wuss!"

"Mama, can I please go now?"

Mama's forehead flushed pink, the way it did when she felt something deeply. "Okay, sugar," she said. "Where'd you say you're going?"

"Just . . . just a bike ride."

Her mother's pink forehead said, *A bike ride? Instead of a movie together?* But she gave a quick nod and headed for the couch, where she flopped down, switched on the fan, and held a magazine in front of her face.

"Ride carefully," she said.

. . .

Before she left, Gladys changed into a clean tee and her bib overalls. She didn't have the heart for anything more stylish, though she did add some bangle bracelets. She tucked her allowance into the front pocket, in case by some miracle she ran into Chickie and got invited to Scoops, and then, at the last minute, she also tucked in the paint scraper. Not that she expected to see Jude. Jude the Rude. But just in case.

She rode her bike aimlessly, fretting over True. Jude said it was no use going back there. She couldn't commit a dognapping, after all. And it was wrong to give True false hope.

But could any hope be completely false? Hope was about possibility, and who could know for sure what was possible?

She remembered how True had picked up her green velvet hat. What if she'd been waiting for Gladys to come back for it? Maybe she'd been sitting by the doghouse or pacing the yard, listening for Gladys's footsteps. Whenever someone walked by, she'd peer through the fence, hoping it was Gladys. If True hadn't given up on Gladys, how could Gladys give up on her?

This time, when their eyes met, Gladys would know what to do.

She fingered the paint scraper. It had a nice, menacing edge. It would make a good weapon, not that Gladys believed in weapons.

At the corner of Seventh Street she got off her bike, wanting to be as inconspicuous as possible when she approached the house. While she considered whether to hide the bike in the bushes where Sophie had pooped, a familiar voice rang out.

"Munchkin!"

Her old third-grade teacher, Mrs. Marsh, pulled up in her

car. Mrs. Marsh called everyone munchkin, so Gladys didn't take it personally.

"How are you?" Mrs. Marsh beamed. "Are you having a good summer? I love your bangle bracelets, by the way. What brings you to my street?"

"Nothing. I mean . . ."

Gladys looked past the car to True Blue's house. In the yard, nothing moved except the tips of the pine tree, nodding in an invisible breeze.

"I mean," she said, "I just decided to go for an impromptu bike ride."

"Impromptu." Mrs. Marsh dimpled. "You and your wonderful vocabulary!"

"I was on my way home, but then I noticed that house. The one with the pine tree?"

"That place." Mrs. Marsh sighed. "It's a revolving door. Nobody rents it long enough for us to get to know them."

"Who lives there now?"

"There was a fellow with a motorcycle. We hardly ever saw him except when he was out in the yard, playing with his dog. Then his girlfriend, must be, moved in, but I don't think they got along." Mrs. Marsh frowned. "Anyway, to make a long story short, I haven't seen that motorcycle for a while now." She shook her head, looking morose. "When I think what this town used to be, people living here for generations, and how it's changed!"

"So now the girlfriend lives there alone? With the dog?"

Mrs. Marsh rested her forearm on the car's open window and gave Gladys a curious look.

"Why are you so interested, munchkin?"

"I just . . . I think I've seen her walking the dog. And it doesn't look happy."

"I don't think it is." Mrs. Marsh pursed her lips. She was wearing burnt orange lipstick, to match her top. Back in third grade, Gladys hadn't yet developed her fashion sense, but she'd always loved how Mrs. Marsh dressed. "How's Celeste?" she asked, meaning Chickie. "Are you two still friends?"

Why was she asking that all of a sudden? Gladys nodded.

"Please answer in a complete sentence."

"Celeste and I are still friends."

"Good. I'm happy to hear that, Gladys. Everybody needs a friend! Now go on and enjoy your impromptu bike ride. There's not much summer left. Don't waste it!"

"Bye, Mrs. Marsh."

Mrs. Marsh had always warned the class she had eyes in the back of her head, and she'd proven it many times. Gladys had no choice but to climb on her bike and pretend to ride away.

At the corner, she stopped and looked back. Mrs. Marsh's car was in her driveway. Nobody was in sight. Gladys rode back and stashed her bike in the bushes. Her heart was beating too fast. Did a chicken's heart beat like this? Was that where the phrase *chicken heart* came from? She flattened her hand against it, trying to calm it down.

Maybe she had other things wrong with her, but Gladys was not a quitter.

She slipped across the street, ducking behind a parked car. Being small could be an advantage sometimes.

But when she peered around the car, she saw that one of the lawn chairs was tipped over in the driveway. In the yard, the wash line was still tethered to the doghouse, but the other end lay in the dirt. Resting beside it was her green velvet hat.

Where was True?

Beneath the pine tree, where the ground was littered with pine cones and pine-cone-like turds, a wreath of gray smoke rose. The tree's thick trunk bulged as another thinner, smaller tree detached itself. The witch lady. How long had she been there? She pulled on her cigarette like it was food.

Gladys watched her untie the wash line and slowly coil it. She threw her cigarette on the ground, then kicked one of True's dishes. After that she just stood there, head to one side like it was a burden too heavy to bear. Gladys waited, and still True's owner stood there. She stood there so long that Gladys began to fear she really had turned to wood, the nightmare come true.

Jude

S he's back!" Spider busted into the bathroom where Jude was working. "I saw her out the window!"

Jude went to the living room and cracked the front blinds. Gladys was hopping from foot to foot like she had to pee or her shoes were on fire. She was holding—was that his paint scraper? He undid the locks and opened the door.

"Just to be clear, I'm ready to be magnan—generous. I forgive you for being rude to my mother." Breathing hard, she had red spots on both cheeks. She must have ridden that dinky excuse for a bike as fast as it could go. She waved his paint scraper around. "Also, I know you claim you don't want to help True—"

"I don't *claim*. I—"

"But you should know that she's gone missing."

"What?" He grabbed the paint scraper before she did any damage. "How do you know?"

She took that for an invitation and barged in. Standing in the living room, she pulled deep breaths through her nose, like she was doing that mindfulness junk they taught at school. It didn't seem to be working.

"Yikes," she said. "I never saw so many doilies in my life."

"A lady at Good Sam makes them. That's where my mother works."

"Really? My grandmother was there before she died. It wasn't a very nice place." She pulled another breath, this one so deep he was afraid she'd inflate. "I'm sorry. I know your mother's nice."

"No she's not. I keep trying to tell you that." He couldn't believe she'd come here. He'd figured her for the kind who stuck to her guns and stayed mad. "What do you mean the dog's gone?"

She took off her bike helmet and her hair exploded.

"Where's Soapie?" demanded Spider. "You didn't bring Soapie?"

"Not today, buddy."

He snatched the bike helmet from her and ran out of the room.

Her shoes—weren't those what people wore for bowling? When she sat down they didn't even touch the floor. One corner of the love seat was ripped up from when Spider experimented with Mom's razor, so Jude had to sit closer than he wanted.

"Are you going to tell me or what?"

"I went back there. She's gone. All I saw was the woman." Gladys grabbed a doily, wadded it up between her hands. Smoothed it out, then immediately wadded it back up. "I had a nightmare about her. It was like a myth where someone gets trapped inside a rock or a tree. The living being is still in there, silently howling, begging to be released, but no one can tell." She shut her eyes for a second. "It was one of the creepiest dreams I've ever had, and I've had lots of really bad dreams."

"You have?"

She nodded.

That was a surprise.

"Trees aren't creepy," he said. "You are dissing trees."

"It was my subconscious! I can't help it. There was another part, too, where I leaned over and…Never mind! When I saw her just now, it was like the nightmare was coming true." She beat her heels against the sofa and one of her bowling shoes fell off. "I waited and watched but she just stood there. She's lost her mind or her heart or her soul or I don't know what. Mrs. Marsh told me her boyfriend took off and left True behind. Do you think that's what made her so mean? Him leaving her?"

"Maybe," he said. "But she could've been mean before and that's why he left. Not that it matters."

He was pretty sure Gladys thought it did matter, but she didn't argue, which wasn't like her at all.

"Sometimes this thing happens where trees, they turn into stone." He took the doily from her and put it back on the armrest. "Petrified, it's called. There's a whole national park called the Petrified Forest. They got ginkgoes there that are like two hundred million years old, turned to solid stone."

"Are you saying she's a petrified human? That's a really good metaphor."

"I bet Pookie ran away. Saw her chance and took off. She's probably out there right now running free as the wind. Who could blame her, right?" When Gladys didn't answer, he went on, "Or maybe the petrified woman gave her away. Or drove her someplace and dumped her."

"Jude! Don't even say that!"

"People do bad stuff." It felt like it was up to him to tell her that. Like he had to inform her the rest of the world wasn't so wonderful as she thought. It didn't make him feel good, though. And it only made her mad. She beat her heels and the other shoe fell off.

"She could be scared and hungry. Possibly sick or injured.

111

And all alone in the universe." Her too-big eyes filled with tears. "*We* know how exceptional she is, but other people might just see a stray with a horrible bark." She grabbed the doily back and swiped her cheek. "They won't care about her."

Spider tore in and out of the room, wearing her bike helmet and making motorcycle noises. Jude thought of how, even after Ms. Suza saw what a massive pain Spider could be, she told them to come back again. Like she knew there was a different kid, a lovable kid, hidden inside Spy. All of a sudden, Jude got why Gladys was here. She was just like her mother! Two peas in a pod. No matter how hard Jude tried to convince her that he didn't want anything to do with True-Pookie, Gladys refused to listen. She just kept right on believing there was another kid stuck inside him. A kid brave or determined or loco enough to care about a dog nobody else did.

"Even if someone does try to help True, she won't trust them," Gladys was saying. "Why should she? All people do is let her down." She stared at her socks. "Including me."

Spider rode his invisible motorcycle over the coffee table and back out of the room. Jude had an idea.

"What about the pound? Maybe somebody turned her in."

"I should've thought of that." She pulled out her phone, got the town's website, and called animal control. Listened. Tapped the phone. Listened. Hung up looking disgusted.

"That was a recording! There's no more department of animal control. It was eliminated due to *budget constraints*." She drilled her finger into the ripped cushion. "I detest when people misuse language for evil purposes. Like my father's auto plant got *unallocated*? No! It got *shut down* and everyone got *fired*! The town decided animals aren't as important as other things.

Why don't they just admit it?" She probed that cushion like maybe the answer was down there.

"Just as well," he said. "If they put her in a cage she'd bark her head off. Who'd adopt a freaked-out dog with funky eyes and a triangle head? She'd probably just get put to sleep. In other words, killed."

If there was a word that meant sad all the way through, like, saturated with sad, that was how she looked.

He stood up. That kind of sadness was contagious.

She folded her hands. Bit her lip. Gave herself a shake. When she put her shoes back on, she tied them with double knots. Then she stood up, too.

"It's up to us to find her," she said. Before he could even open his mouth, she said, "You need to help me, Jude. I don't think I can do this alone."

"I would, okay? You're right. I get it. Pookie shouldn't be out there all scared and alone. She got a really bad deal. She deserves way better. But I'm on lockdown." He heard how fast he was talking. Heard his mother saying, *Don't give me those sorry lame excuses.* "I got this bathroom to paint, my brother to watch. I—I got my summer reading and math to do."

Gladys put her hands on her hips. Her bracelets made a noise like silverware when you slam the drawer.

"Besides," he said, "Pookie could be anyplace. She could be in the next county. It'd be a miracle if you found her and guess what? I do not believe in miracles."

"This is the most I've ever heard you speak," she said.

"I'm done."

She circled the room, then stopped directly in front of him. Hooked her thumbs in her overall straps.

"How about we make a deal?" she said. "I help you finish the bathroom and you help me look for True."

He leaned back. Mom was working a double shift. She wouldn't be home till late. If he didn't have to worry about Spider, he could get a lot done. And if Gladys worked her juju on Spider, he wouldn't rat on them.

"You really want to watch my brother?"

"I said I'd help you finish the bathroom!"

"That's how you can help."

She gritted her teeth. "You might not have noticed, but I actually can't stand little kids. Nevertheless, I'll do whatever it takes."

How'd a person get like that? If somebody asked him to define a Gladys, he'd say a person small and stubborn as a fire hydrant. She wouldn't give up. Not on True. Not on him.

But being stubborn was only a good thing if you were right. Otherwise, it was a big mistake.

Big.

"One hour," he said.

"And a half."

"Okay. You keep Spider out of my way that long, and I'll help you look."

"Deal! But I get to go first." She turned and called, "Spider! Where are you, buddy?"

He zoomed into the room, wearing her helmet and revving his invisible motorcycle. Jude followed them to the front door. The sun shone a spotlight on his murdered white pine.

What was he getting himself into?

114

Gladys

They stopped at every corner, cupping their hands and calling.

"True! Don't be scared, girl!" Gladys.

"Pookie! Get your butt over here." Jude.

"I'm hot. I'm thirsty. I'm hot. I'm thirsty." Spider.

Gladys had left her bike at Jude's house and needed to take three steps for every one of his. When they got to the old elementary school, now a drug clinic, he grabbed Spider's hand and pulled him past. Some scruffy guys leaned against the parking lot fence. A woman slept on a bench, a bulging garbage bag at her feet. Whenever Gladys went by here, she fixed her eyes straight ahead. But Jude sped up as if the people were dangerous.

"Slow down!" she begged, struggling to keep up.

"I can't stand looking at those losers." Anger rose off him like steam.

"Kicking addiction is very difficult. Only an extremely small percentage of users manage to do it."

"It's their fault, getting addicted in the first place."

Mama said people who went to the clinic were at least trying. They deserved respect, and the ones who didn't quit, who couldn't, deserved compassion. Gladys's birth mother, she meant. Mama had talked Gladys through this again and again. Gladys could have given Jude a whole lecture on the subject of addiction, but for one thing, keeping pace with him was using most of her available oxygen and for another, why push her luck? He was already in a foul enough mood.

"It's not useful to blame people," she said. Also a Mama quote, but shorter.

"What do you mean?"

"It doesn't help. It doesn't change whatever went wrong or whatever bad choice they made. The only way to do that is learn from their mistake."

His expression turned pensive.

The late-afternoon sun beat down and the sidewalk sizzled. Spider climbed a fire escape before they could stop him, pounded his chest, and climbed back down. The few people they passed regarded them with varying degrees of pity and disdain. No, they hadn't seen a shaggy multicolored dog. No, they hadn't heard barking that sounded like somebody shaking a bucket full of nails. Gladys's hope began to ebb. Maybe the petrified woman had given True away. But what if True had run away? Skittish as she was, she might not stop till she was so lost she'd never find her way back. She could have gotten hit by a car and be lying on the side of some road. She could be dead.

Gladys stopped walking. Jude was almost to the train tracks, but he turned around, scowling.

"What?" he called back.

She couldn't let him know she was losing hope. He'd say I told you so and head straight home. Then what would she do?

"My shoe." She pretended to tie it, then scurried to catch up.

The afternoon shadows were growing longer and she wondered, where would True go once it got dark? Would she find a safe place? When you were as small as Gladys was, the world always seemed too big, but now, right now, it seemed bigger than ever before. There was too much world. It could swallow down a lost, scared creature without a trace.

True, remember when you told me you were looking for someone? Well, now I'm looking for you!

Gladys's shoulders ached. Her feet grew leaden and her throat parched. Jude was already at the tracks, impatiently waiting for her. Gladys had never crossed the tracks, except inside a car. She wasn't allowed. Not that she'd ever wanted to go there. Now she forced a smile, trying to appear nonchalant instead of worried sick.

Jude

He could see she was never going to give up. *Never.* They'd search all night, all week, all month. They'd search till Christmas and she still wouldn't give up.

Jude had never met anybody with that much faith in herself. That much faith in the world.

Faith in *him.*

It made him itch, like a rash.

She needed to quit smiling. Her face was too small for a smile that wide. She was going to bust a muscle and the smile would slide off, *splat* on the sidewalk.

He should say he was done. Her time was up and now she owed him. He should tell her.

They crossed the tracks into no-man's-land. Gladys swiveled her head like danger lurked on every side. Still, she made it all the way to the scrapyard before saying they better turn around.

Spider went boneless, so Jude had to put him on his shoulders. They were almost back to the tracks when the lights started flashing. His little brother dug his fingers into Jude's skull.

"Train!" he shouted.

Wait.

Wait.

Gladys caught up to them. "You hear that?" he asked her.

"The train? I'm not deaf."

The whistle—two long, one short, another long. The train was getting closer, bigger, louder. Still, Jude heard something else. He ran up the berm, leaned through the barriers.

"What are you doing?" Gladys squeaked. "Get back!"

Across the tracks, a short, heavy man stepped out of the alley beside Freddy's Bar and Grill. He was dragging Pookie on a rope. On his shoulder, where a soldier rests his gun, was a golf club.

"We're coming!" Jude shouted.

"Don't!" Gladys grabbed his arm. "It's too close!"

Even over the noise of the train, Pookie heard them. She went up on her hind legs, twisted her head, gave a strangled bark. The man's face—Freddy, it was Freddy—darkened. He raised his golf club. The train thundered across the tracks.

Spider shouted the name of every car. "*Box! Hopper! Open!*"

The longest freaking freight train in the world.

Gladys

People said if you got too close to a speeding train it would suck you into its vortex. Ground meat, that was your fate. Gladys had never quite believed it, but now she felt something pulling Jude, pulling so hard she needed to hold on to him with all her might.

It was True, not the train. True was calling him just the way she'd called Gladys.

"Caboose!" Spider shouted as Jude swung him down from his shoulders and took off, ducking under the barriers, flying across the tracks. Grabbing Spider's hand, Gladys raced after him. The rails still hummed. The heat bit her skin.

True and Freddy were nowhere in sight.

They ran down the alleyway. Trash cans overflowed with empty chip bags and ketchup-streaked napkins, and the smell of beer and burgers seeped through the screen door. Cautiously peering inside, Gladys spotted Freddy behind the bar where a guy in a delivery uniform hunched over a glass of beer. The TV on the wall played the baseball game. True was nowhere in sight.

"This damn town!" Freddy said. The delivery man looked more interested in his beer. "I swear on my mother's grave, it's circling the drain."

"Hey," Jude was whispering. Gladys turned to see him

peeking under a wooden bench a few feet from the door. "Hey you."

A rope was tied around one leg of the bench. When Gladys crouched beside Jude, she saw True's blue eyes staring back at them. She had to clap her hand over her mouth to keep from shouting with happiness.

"It's us!" she whispered between her fingers.

True cowered, pressing herself against the brick of the building. When Gladys reached toward her, the fur along her spine shot up in a ridge. She bared her fangs, showing her spotted gums. A growl deep in her throat made Gladys skitter back, heart knocking against her ribs.

"He'll bite you!" Spider cried. "He'll rip you up!"

"Quiet!" Jude warned his brother. He knelt down and untied the rope from the bench.

"She's too scared," Gladys whispered. "She won't come out."

"Keep an eye on the door," he ordered.

Gladys sidled over and spied through the screen. Freddy was getting more agitated.

"I got a mangy mutt knocking over trash cans, crapping in my alley," he told the delivery man. "Like my business isn't already in trouble? One of my customers tried to pet it and it almost bit her."

"It bit her?" The man finally looked up.

"Not actually but . . ."

Jude was kneeling beside the bench, one hand on the ground and the other resting on his thigh. Spider tugged at him, whining and trying to pull him back, but Jude pushed his brother away. Jude looked different, from up above. Gladys could literally see another side of him, and not just literally but also . . . also whatever the opposite of literally was. Her breath caught in her throat as he slowly extended one hand, keeping it flat to the ground. True's nose poked out and sniffed it. Her whimper was a question. Gladys remembered how Jude had soothed little Mateo into a deep, peaceful sleep. How he'd let his gentle out from wherever he kept it hidden.

"I called animal control and guess what?" Freddy's voice rose. Glancing back, Gladys saw him pick up his golf club and tap his open palm. "No more animal control."

"That's a dirty shame," the delivery man said.

"Looks like I have to take matters into my own hands," Freddy stepped out from behind the bar. "That mutt's going on a long car ride."

"Jude!" Gladys said. "Hurry!"

As True eased out from under the bench, Spider backed away, eyes huge. "The spooky dog!" He scrambled up onto a metal trash can, which fell over with a clang that echoed up and down the alley. Garbage flew. Spider hit the ground with a shout. Gladys saw Freddy charge toward the door, clutching the golf club.

"He's coming!"

True was off like a shot. Somehow Jude managed to catch hold of her rope and race after her.

"Grab Spider!" Jude yelled.

Gladys caught Spider's hand and they ran, too, skidding on trash and knocking elbows as the screen door banged open and Freddy burst through. Throwing a look over her shoulder, Gladys saw a slash of metal and a face the color of uncooked meat.

"What the hell?" Freddy cried.

Spider might whine like a mosquito but he ran like a

jackrabbit. They burst out of the alley into the sunshine of the street and kept on going. When she dared to look back again, Gladys saw Freddy leaning on the golf club.

"Thanks, whoever you are!" he hollered. "Good riddance to bad rubbish!"

Jude disappeared around the corner. When she and Spider caught up, he was behind the old toy store, huffing and puffing.

"I should go back and pop that guy," he said.

"I agree, but please don't."

Gladys had seen Jude angry before. He was angry at least half the time. But this was different. The anger was rolling off him in big, crashing waves. Spider leaned against her and slid his thumb in his mouth, and she knew he felt his brother's anger, too.

"It doesn't matter," she told Jude. "You saved her." True smelled awful, like pee and garbage. She was panting, her skinny sides heaving. Gladys longed to touch her but didn't dare. "Poor girl," she said. "Poor thing."

"Don't say that."

"What?"

"She's brave. She ran away. You got what you wanted, didn't you, Pook?"

One ear went up. Something flickered in those beautiful blue eyes, and Gladys thought of trick birthday candles that, no matter how many times you tried to blow them out, lit up again.

"It's gonna bite you, Jude," Spider said, but by now even he didn't seem to believe that.

Up went the other ear. Each was a perfect triangle, except for the notch in the left one. True nosed Jude's fingers, then closed her eyes and breathed a soft doggy sigh.

Gladys and Jude looked at each other.

"We found her," he said, voice full of wonder.

"Of course we did!" she said, voice full of joy.

He grinned. A smile so big, it was a smile and a half. They'd found her. Gladys was a helium balloon, rising into the glorious, golden, late-day sunlight.

Till Spider asked, "Where you taking it?"

Back to earth sank Gladys.

Jude

Jude kept hold of the rope tied to Pookie's collar. She didn't look like she wanted to run away, but what did he know about dogs?

They smuggled her behind a building that used to be a church, then a dance studio, then a store where ladies sold stuff they knitted. It was empty now, waiting for the next person with a lame business idea. There was a parking lot, a sassafras tree, and a picnic table. Gladys went to the corner store and used her allowance to buy an aluminum pie pan and a jug of water.

No matter how many times Jude filled the pan, Pookie emptied it. That might explain all the peeing.

"Obviously we're not returning her," Gladys said. "So we need a safe place to keep her. Do you have any ideas?"

"Me?" He blinked. "I thought *you* had a plan."

"Well." She poured out more water and they watched Pookie lap it up. "I never said that."

He couldn't believe it.

"The main thing," she said, "was to find her and we did."

"How's that the main thing? That's like…like you plant something, right? It's cool. You feel good. Then you realize you gotta take care of the plant or tree or whatever for the rest of its life. *That's* the main thing."

Gladys drew in her pointy chin. And then, weird and freaky as ever, she smiled at him.

"I just want to say. You were magnificent back there."

Magnificent? Jude's face got hot. He bent to scratch Pookie between the ears. Dogs were supposed to like that, right?

"You're just saying that so I'll keep helping you," he said. "Even though your time is way up."

"Fine. Reject my compliment. But Freddy and his golf club scared me half to death. I'm not used to confrontation. If it wasn't for you, I'd have choked. True wouldn't be here." She clasped her little hands. "And you're absolutely right. We found her, and now she's our responsibility. It's true. True! Her fate is in our hands, Jude."

Pookie tilted her head, directing him where to scratch. When he stopped, she raised an eyebrow till he started up again. This dog! She said whole sentences without talking.

"Jude," Gladys said. He wished she'd quit saying his name. "I didn't exactly think things through, I admit. The fact is, I can't keep her. My mother—" Just as she said this, her phone pinged with a text. She bit her lip. "Speaking of. She'd make us return True right away. Even if by some wild chance I could convince her we should keep True, we couldn't. She's too skittish to be around sprouts. Also, my father is severely allergic." She stuck her hands in her overall pockets. "So it's up to you. If she understood the circumstances, would your mother let you keep her?"

"Oh man," he said. "Oh wow."

"No? Is that a no?"

"I already told you. I never liked dogs. But you know who hates them? Hates them like, if she could, she'd ship every last dog on Earth to Siberia or maybe Mars?"

"Our mom," said Spider, who'd climbed into a crook of the sassafras. Still wearing Gladys's pink bike helmet.

"So even if it was okay to do finders-keepers with a dog," Jude went on, "and even if the owner wouldn't go ballistic if she found out, no. No way."

"But your mother's so nice. Maybe…"

"She's not nice, okay? Your mother's nice. Get it straight."

Her phone pinged with another text. She answered, then sat on the picnic table. Spider was ripping leaves off the tree and throwing them. One, shaped like a mitten, drifted down to stick in her crazy hair. Like the tree had decided to give her a crown.

Who knew how this girl's mind worked? All of a sudden, out of nowhere, she said, "I'm adopted."

That surprised him so much, all he could manage was, "What?"

Her shoulders twitched like he'd thrown something at her.

"Never mind," she said.

"I just—"

"I said, never mind!"

Pookie trotted over to the same patch of grass and peed again.

"Jude," Gladys said. Would she ever quit saying his name? "I can't take her. You can't take her. That means we need a place to hide her, at least temporarily, till we figure out our next step."

He wanted to tell her to quit saying *we*, too.

"A nice safe place where no one will find her," Gladys said.

"We got a secret fortress," Spider said. "Me and Jude and Jabari."

"Really?" Gladys peered up at him. "Where?"

"You're so into vocabulary!" Jude cried. "You don't know what *secret* means?"

"Jude, like it or not, we are in this together."

"I was trying to mind my own business and stay out of trouble. But every time I turn around, there you are."

"You came to my house last time, in case you're suffering a memory lapse."

"That was Spy's idea."

"*And* you came with me today," Gladys went on. "Your actions speak louder than your words. Which isn't surprising, since you act like talking to me is torture."

"Could you even shut up for one minute?"

Pookie whined. Tugged on the rope like she was trying to get away.

"Now look what you did!" Gladys shot him the evil eye. "You scared her!"

"Me?!"

"Yes you. Now are you happy?"

Pookie bent her legs but didn't lie down. She froze like that, halfway between staying and running. Trembling. Something told him, *Don't look her in the eye. Not yet. Wait. Wait till she's ready.* Probably that woman and her boyfriend used to fight. Pookie had to listen to them shouting, saying horrible stuff to each other. Listen and not know what to do.

"Hey," he told her softly. "Hey. I know."

His hand was on her head. It was running down her back, gentle but firm. Again. Then again. Spider watched, sucking his thumb. Up in the tree, he looked little. He *was* little. That was easy to forget, with all the massive trouble he caused. He still hadn't come near the dog, and Jude knew he was afraid.

It's a dog, it bites.

Jude had stopped being afraid without even noticing. How'd that happen?

"You can pet her," he told his brother.

Spider shook his head. You couldn't make someone trust. It took time. They had to find their own way to it.

Slowly, Pookie eased herself down, deciding not to run. Deciding to stay, at least for now.

Trusting him.

When Jude looked up, that girl was watching him with her too-big eyes. A leaf-crown on her head.

"So we can use your secret fort?" she asked.

Gladys

Back at the store Gladys used the rest of her allowance for another pan and a bag of dog food. Who knew kibble cost so much? If only she had enough money to buy a proper leash, too, and a brush for True's matted fur. Money, that was another thing she hadn't exactly thought through.

She hurried back to the old church, but stopped as she rounded the corner of the building. Jude sat on the ground, resting his back against the tree. To one side of him was True, asleep with her head on her paws, and to his other side was Spider. Jude must've finally persuaded him to take off the bike helmet, and he was asleep with his head in his big brother's lap.

Jealousy pricked her. All right, more than pricked—stabbed. She'd never minded being an only child, and she didn't like little kids, but the way Spider slumped against Jude, trusting him so completely you could tell he'd done it all his life, ever since he was born ... All of a sudden, that seemed like a thing to envy.

And look at True! She trusted him, too. Jude was the one who'd already figured out where she liked to be scratched, who knew how to stop her trembling and barking.

How had that happened?

Gladys hugged the kibble bag. *Stab stab* went the knife of

130

jealousy. Things were not going the way she'd pictured. Jude was absolutely right. Saving True had been all her idea! She'd had to force him to help her. She'd thought . . . Well, maybe she'd never actually *thought* it, since Jude was also right that she didn't have a completely organized plan. But she'd imagined True liking *her*. Not just liking her. Loving her. Not just loving her. Loving her best in all the world.

Instead, what if True picked Jude to love? What if even True could tell something was wrong with her?

I'm adopted. Why did she tell Jude that? What made her blurt it out? The second she did, she'd wanted to un-tell him. He'd reacted as if she'd confessed she had a contagious disease. *What?* he'd said, as if he felt sorry for her.

Now he looked up to find her watching him. Embarrassed and annoyed, she marched across the parking lot.

"There's a problem," he said.

"You can't go back on your word! You promised to take her to the fortress."

"The thing is." He shielded Spider's ear, as if his little brother could hear even in his sleep. "The thing is, I can't take Spy with me. The fortress is where he got hurt. I swore to my mother I'd never take him back there."

"Why don't I like the sound of this?"

"Your mom said he was welcome at your house anytime, remember?"

She sat beside him. "Let me get this straight. You want to take True by yourself? Without me?"

He nodded.

This was so extremely unfair. Not to mention, how could she let Jude take True to a place she'd never seen? A supposed fortress? She needed to check it out herself. She needed to supervise. Even though by now it was so late her mother would be having a fit.

"It's across the tracks."

"What?"

"Nobody knows about it except me and my friend Jabari. Maybe you've seen him at school. Skinny dude with a birthmark? He's actually not my friend anymore, but we swore never to tell anyone, and Jabari, he'd never break a swear. So it's a safe place."

"Safe? It's definitely not safe across the tracks."

"The fortress is different."

The way he described it now, she imagined a shining castle with turrets and flags, which was ridiculous, but still. They'd been building it all summer, he said, and nobody ever bothered them. He made it sound like the place radiated its own magical force field, deflecting all harm. Nobody lived nearby, he said. It was a secret fortress. *Secret.*

"I'll make sure she's okay," he said. True yawned an extravagant yawn, then settled her head on his knee.

Gladys squeezed her eyes shut. She saw him in the alleyway behind Freddy's, patiently coaxing True out from under the bench. She gritted her teeth.

"I guess I'll have to trust you."

"You will?"

She opened her eyes in time to see an arrow of joy shoot across his face. A heartbeat later, Gladys felt it pierce her.

Ow.

She held True's rope as Jude woke Spider, who was grouchy in that way of all just-waked sprouts. But when Jude told him he was going to Ms. Suza's house, he jumped up, ready. True jumped up, too, alert and watchful, ears cocked, tail slowly sweeping the air.

"Jude's going to take you to a new place," Gladys told her. "You'll be safe there, don't worry. We won't let anyone hurt you ever again, I promise. Jude promises, too. He even said it out loud which in case you haven't noticed yet is really unusual for him."

Gladys and Jude put their numbers into each other's phones. They agreed that since Jude's mother was off from work tomorrow, Gladys would go to the fortress to take care of True. Jude didn't have an address for the place, but he gave her directions as best he could.

At last, she handed him the dog's rope, and he gave her Spider's hand. A miserable trade! But then, all of a sudden, like a magician producing a coin, Jude plucked something from her hair.

"Sassafras," he said, handing her a leaf.

It was shaped like a mitten. If it really was a mitten, it would've fit her hand perfectly.

He hoisted the bag of dog food, and she watched them walk away. True Blue for Spider. Spider for True Blue. It was the worst deal of Gladys's life, but what choice did she have?

Jude

Jude walked fast, keeping an eye out for the petrified woman. Once some kids on skateboards rumbled by, making Pookie bark and tremble and pee the sidewalk, and once a car slowed down and a prune-face woman called out the window, "Your dog needs a bath, young man!" But otherwise, they didn't see anybody.

Your dog.

The closer they got to the fortress, the calmer Pookie got. She trusted him.

That made two creatures—one kooky animal, one freaky human—in the same day.

Jude smiled.

Gladys

It took approximately half a century to go back and retrieve her bike from Jude's house, then ride Spider to hers. She texted Mama to explain that some unusual circumstances had arisen, but she was on the way.

Her mother was pacing the front yard, phone in hand. Sometimes, the best way to describe a thing is to say what it is not.

As in, Mama was not happy.

"Finally." She gave Gladys the we'll-deal-with-this-later look, then turned her attention to Spider. "Look who's here. All by himself. Wearing my daughter's bike helmet." Mama lifted Spider from the bike seat. "It's past suppertime. Someone looks hungry and thirsty."

With Gladys's mother, sprouts always came first. In the kitchen she wiped Spider's face and hands with a soft, warm cloth. She set him at the table with a glass of milk and a plate of mac and cheese. Dada, she said, had already eaten, then gone to help a neighbor plant a tree in his yard.

"What kind of tree?" Gladys asked, a feeble effort to distract her mother.

"I do not have that information." Mama handed her a plate, too, and Gladys meekly sank into a chair.

"Brown noodles are gross," Spider said, shoveling in the whole wheat pasta. "Where's my BFF?"

"Not here today, buddy," Mama said.

Mama didn't believe in discussing sprouts in front of them. Even babies understood when you were talking about them, she said. She waited till Spider had polished off a second plate and they'd all gone into the backyard, where Spider jumped onto a big wheel, to fold her arms and ask what was going on.

"For starters, where's Jude? Who, by the way, I thought you were angry at?"

"He . . . he had something he really wanted to do. Something important. He couldn't do it if he had to bring Spider. So I said I'd watch him for a while."

Please please don't ask what Jude had to do.

She watched her mother consider. Considerate, that was Mama.

"And their mom?"

"She's working at Good Sam."

It was Mama's mother who'd been at Good Sam before she died. Her eyes clouded.

"You said Spider was welcome here anytime," Gladys reminded her. "I didn't think you'd mind. I'll take responsibility. I'll make sure he doesn't climb the swing set."

Spider had already abandoned the big wheel for the slide, which he scrambled up backward and leaped off approximately a hundred times. Watching him, Mama's expression softened. Her look seesawed between sympathy and amusement. Difficult kids were her specialty. They were knots she untied, puzzles she solved. Gladys felt a sudden, dangerous surge of love for her mother. Who, as if she felt it, turned with a small smile.

"That was nice of you, sugar," she said. "That was a generous, good-friend thing to do."

Gladys picked up a strip of tree bark fallen in the grass and pretended to examine it. The tree had weird, scaly bark, as if an incompetent wizard had tried to conjure up a reptile but gotten a tree instead.

"I know this hasn't been the best summer for you, and I'm sorry about that," Mama went on. "But even so, you're trying to help others. That makes me proud and happy."

Gladys prayed her mother couldn't see the guilt seeping out all around her edges.

"I don't expect you to tell me everything anymore. Lord knows I kept secrets when I was your age. Not dangerous secrets, of course. But there were lots of things only my diary knew." Mama rubbed her forehead. "Promise next time you go visit Jude or anyone else, you'll tell me where you are."

"Okay." Gladys nervously broke off little bits of the bark. Mama's face got an unusual, wistful look.

"You know, speaking of Good Sam—I've been thinking lately about how often your grandma and I didn't get along. She was always after me, nagging me to be more ambitious. I think she wanted me to have a better life than she did. Well, all mothers want that. But her criticism hurt. It made me angry, too. I was ambitious, just not the way Ma wanted."

Gladys had never heard this story before. She looked up.

"The worst argument we ever had—I mean, World War Three—was when I told her I was going to marry Dada. She said I was making the biggest mistake of my life."

"How could she say that?" Gladys cried. "Couldn't she see you and Dada were perfect for each other?"

"I guess not." Mama pinched the skin above her nose. "He'd never amount to much, Ma said. But I already knew how much he loved me, and that was all that mattered. I guess it came down to different definitions of the word *much*." She started to bite her thumbnail, then folded her thumb into her fist. "This will sound terrible, but if she'd been alive when Dada lost his job at the plant, she might've blamed him. I can hear her now. *See, Suzanna? I told you so.*"

"Mama! You never told me this."

"I know, sugar. Maybe I shouldn't even tell you now. One thing for sure, your grandma adored you." Mama gazed across the yard at Spider, who was wandering toward the garage. "I didn't want to spoil that for either one of you."

Gladys didn't know what to say. Her grandmother was Mama's birth mother! How could they be so different?

"I wish I could've made her happier, I really do, but I never figured out how." Mama sighed, then smiled. "Lucky for you and me, we don't have that problem."

Gladys got busy with the tree bark again.

"Sugar, whenever there's something you need to talk about, I'm here to listen. Don't ever be afraid to—aack!"

With a burst of superhuman speed, Mama was flying across the yard. She was grabbing a pair of hedge clippers out of Spider's hands.

"Where did you even find these?" Mama, who almost never yelled, yelled. Spider sprinted for the swing set.

"My mom has some, too." He shinnied up the pole but Mama plucked him off.

"Clippers are dangerous, Spider. You could hurt yourself. You could hurt someone else."

"You smack me and I'll tell Jude!"

"I am not going to smack you. I'm going to keep you safe." She bent to look him in the eye. "Someday you'll be big

138

enough to use clippers, but not yet. You understand? Do you understand, Spider?"

He stretched out on the grass and did his corpse imitation.

"You're tired, aren't you?" Mama asked.

"No."

Mama picked him up and he sagged against her. When babies were first born, they understood nothing. They didn't even understand that they were separate from the rest of the world, so their own arms and legs, waving around, were like random objects that could surprise and scare them. Mama was expert at swaddling babies in soft, fuzzy blankets, tucking their arms and legs close to make them feel whole and safe. Safe and whole. Now her arms made a warm blanket around Spider, who yawned as if she'd swaddled all the chaos straight out of him.

"What's your name?" she asked him.

"Spider."

"Your real name."

"I don't know," he said, and then, "Silas."

"Come on, Silas. Let's go read a story."

A breeze came up, parting the leaves of the reptile tree, and when Gladys lifted her eyes she saw the first star, pale and glimmering. When she was younger, spotting the first star meant *Make a wish*. But then Gladys learned that the stars she saw might have burned up long before. What if she was wishing on something that didn't even exist anymore? That felt like a trick. Like the universe was working a hoax.

The *uniworse*, as Sophie would say.

The breeze lifted the leaves and Gladys saw for the first time how they were smooth on top, hairy and bumpy underneath. Even trees kept secrets. Or tried to.

Gladys pushed open the gate and walked out front. Where was Jude? What was taking him so long? What if he'd gotten cold feet and decided he couldn't handle this rescue after all? What if he'd changed his mind and taken True back to her owner? He could just stick her inside the fence and run. Jude was a pathetic runner, but he could make a getaway.

The first star was growing brighter. What if, instead of a hoax, it was a sign? Too many things and people, once they were gone, they were gone for good. But a star lingered. It shone its light as long as it possibly could, giving you more chances to make a wish.

Where was he?

Gladys closed her eyes and made a wish.

Jude

By the time he and Pookie reached the fortress house, the air was cooling down. No grasshoppers busted out of the grass. A lonely cricket chirped like the last surviving bug on the planet.

Out back, everything looked just the same. Super Soaker in the grass. Plywood knocked sideways. A corner of the tarp caved in. A spiderweb stretched across what was supposed to be the entrance. Much as he loved the fortress, Jabari must have stayed away, too.

Pookie whimpered. Jude nodded.

"Right. I blew it with my best friend."

He tied her to the railing of the back steps, but her legs got tangled in the rope. Jude untangled her. Tangled. Untangled.

"Just sit!" Guess who did? "Wow. You know how to do that?"

Her look said, *You could've asked me before now.* Jude laughed. He set down the aluminum pan, opened the bag of dog food, and poured some out. While she gobbled, he moved the evil board. It was so heavy, he couldn't believe he'd ever picked it up, let alone thrown it. It was like somebody else had done it. He hauled it back behind the garage. No way that board was going to hurt anybody else.

When Pookie had the pan licked clean, she picked it up in her teeth and tossed it over her head. Jude laughed again.

Poured out more kibble and watched that disappear, too. Feeding someone so hungry felt good. Scary, too, because at this rate, they'd need another bag quick, and where was the money for that supposed to come from? Better not think about that now.

Once Pookie polished off the second helping, she stretched her front legs out, butt high. Lifted her head and yawned, then shook herself all over. A paw on his knee, like, *Thanks, dude*.

You're welcome.

Next she got to work sniffing the grass like she was Detective Dog and every blade was a clue. Watching, he must've lost track of time, because next thing he knew, the sky was streaked with pink.

"I gotta go."

Why was he always saying that?

She sat down, wrapped her crooked tail around herself. What she did now, Gladys called it waiting. Lifting her head, looking into the distance. Beaming a message into the universe. *Here I am. Right here. Waiting.*

Her nose twitched. After a while she dipped her snout in a doggy nod. Like she'd settled something. Like, *Okay. I decided.*

Next thing he knew, she was looking at him.

And then she licked his hand.

Whoa.

A lump in his throat. His voice squeaked out around it.

"Okay. Look here." He undid the rope from the railing and led her to the fortress. "It's real peaceful, see? I'll tie you to the fence, but you can go in and out whenever you want to do your business. You can sleep on this deluxe Beautyrest mattress. Best you can buy, Jabari's grandma swears it."

She sniffed the tarp suspiciously. Narrowed her eyes.

"Don't look at me like that, okay? It's safe here. My friend says it's like the fortress of solitude. You ever heard of that?"

He thought of Gladys saying he acted like talking was torture. He thought of Mom warning him never go near a dog, let alone have a conversation with one. He thought, who the freak am I turning into?

"See? I'll show you." He crawled inside, threw himself on the mattress, and sighed like he'd died and gone to heaven. "Sure is wonderful here! Sure wish I could stay here myself!"

He tugged her rope but she wouldn't budge. All right. He'd wait. He'd peel back the edge of the tarp and look at that star. It was the only one in the sky, like all the rest of the stars decided to give it a chance to be the star star. By now the world's last surviving cricket had given up. He could hear Pookie breathing, that's how quiet it was. He tried to match his breath to hers, the way, when he couldn't sleep, he listened to Spider breathing.

Make a wish, his father had told him. Jude closed his eyes.

I wish I could stay here forever.

Something wet poked his arm. He opened his eyes.

Her breath was worse than his backpack that time he forgot a carton of milk in it over spring break. She rested her head on the mattress and lifted her eyes to him.

I wish we both could stay.

When was he going to quit making wishes?

He tried to make his voice calm. Moon-calm, like Ms. Suza's.

"I'm going to fill your water dish again, but then I really gotta go. Gladys is going to come tomorrow. You know, that girl who talks too much? Wears funky clothes?"

He tied the rope to the fence, then crawled out backward. Right away she tried to follow him. Right away her feet tangled

143

up. She whined and bit at the rope, shaking it like a neck she wanted to break.

"Take it easy! I can't bring you home! I just can't."

She didn't get it. How was she supposed to get it? She didn't even know what *home* really meant.

That thought got to him. He had to stop and regroup for a minute.

He carried the pan inside, filled it with water, spilled it going down the steps, went back inside, filled it only halfway, brought it back out, and set it by the fortress entrance. He untangled her feet. Again.

"Just chill, okay?"

The second he walked away, she started barking. He prayed she'd stop when he was out of sight.

Nope. It just got worse, and then she was howling. *Howling.*

He stood at the foot of the driveway.

He had to go.

He had to go.

Jude had spent a lot of time practicing being invisible. Teachers, counselors—he tried to vaporize around them. So when he tiptoed back up the driveway, he didn't make a sound. Top-of-the-line noise-canceling headphones, that's how quiet Jude was.

But she still knew he was coming. She stopped mid-howl. When he poked his head around the corner of the house she was waiting, staring straight at him.

She went up on her back legs and yipped for joy.

I knew it! I knew you wouldn't leave me!

Gladys

Gladys and Spider were playing dinosaurs—meaning his T. rex was attacking her apatosaurus for the umpteenth time—when Jude finally showed up. He looked worn to a nub. Mama tried her best to get him to sit down and have something to eat, but Jude said they needed to go home ASAP.

"Give that back," he told Spider, pointing at the T. rex.

"He can borrow it," Mama said. "He'll bring it back next time, won't you, Silas?"

"No," Spider said.

Dada wanted to drive them home, but Jude said his mother didn't let them take rides with people she'd never met. When they finally escaped her parents' clutches, Gladys followed them out to the sidewalk.

"So? You got her there okay?"

He ran a hand from the back of his head up over the top, and it was as if he'd undone the strings of a mask. Suddenly his face was undefended. Unfortressed. For a terrible moment, Gladys was afraid he'd cry.

"She wouldn't stop barking so I had to put her inside the house." He swallowed. "She's scared. She's freaked."

"And you left her? How could you leave her?"

He stared, as if Gladys had morphed into somebody else.

"Don't!" His voice was fierce as a slap. "Don't blame me!"

"I . . . I didn't mean . . . But what if she keeps barking? And someone hears her? What if someone—"

"What was I supposed to do?" His hands curled into fists.

"You're right. I'm sorry." Gladys was. She truly was sorry, for him and for True Blue. What a mess. A terrible mess and it was just as much her fault as Jude's. Maybe more. But now was not the time to panic.

"We're going to figure this out," she said. "We did the right thing, I'm sure of it. We've got her in a safe place, and she knows we care about her."

"So what?" He socked the tree lawn tree. *Ow!* She felt it in her own knuckles. Wincing, he turned away from her, but not before she saw tears leap into his eyes. He was even more upset than she'd thought.

"So what?" he said again. "Like everything's going to be okay because we *care*?"

He made it sound so stupid.

"Yes," she said, trying to sound sure. "You and me together!"

He clapped his hands over Spider's ears.

"We stole a dog," he whispered.

"We didn't steal her. Anyway . . . anyway *steal* has many meanings. For example, if you steal someone's heart, it's a good thing."

"So what do you call it, Ms. Vocabulary?"

"Rescued."

"Yeah right." He snorted. "Like if that woman finds out, she'll say, Oh, you *rescued* my dog from me? That's kind of *annoying*, but thanks so much!"

"She won't find out. If we're careful, we—"

Spider pulled free of Jude and made the T. rex attack the tree lawn tree. Leaves shaped like little fans drifted down.

"We can't hide her forever," Jude said.

"Obviously," she said.

"What are we supposed to do, hop a freight train and take her somewhere else?"

"Obviously not."

"*Obviously*," he mocked her. "Then? What?"

"You could try to think of something, you know," she said. "Why is it all up to me?"

The T. rex went on a rampage, biting them with its plastic teeth. Jude swung his brother up on his shoulders and started walking.

"Like I told you, my mother's off tomorrow so you need to go."

"I know. I'll be there. No worries." She scurried beside him as he gave her the directions again. "All right. I can find it. But wait. Jude!"

He kept going.

"Jude? This is no time to run amok!"

The T. rex roared.

Jude

He still had time. Mom was working a double shift and wouldn't be home till after eleven. He could give Spider a bath, get him in his PJs, feed him something, and put him to bed. He could even get in a little more work on the bathroom.

He could still get away with this.

Or not.

Her car was in the driveway.

Her car was in the driveway.

Mr. Peters was pacing back and forth in his front yard. By now it was full dark, but his security light lit up his lawn like a landing strip. When he saw Jude and Spider, he threw his hands in the air. His voice rolled out like thunder.

"Thank goodness! Are you two all right? Your mother has been frantic with worry!"

For a moment Jude considered asking Mr. Peters if they could hide out in his house for the rest of their lives. Then he noticed that the driver's door of Mom's car was partway open. When he went to shut it, he saw her purse sitting on the seat.

That massive purse was an extension of her. It was like she'd left her arm behind.

"Jude?" Mr. Peters said. "Will you let me know if I can help?"

Nothing but nothing could help Jude now. Still, as he picked up the purse and ran for the door, he called over his shoulder. "That light? It really fries her nerves."

He threw open the front door, Spider right behind.

"Mom?"

"Thank God!"

She caught hold of them and gave them the once-over, checking for blood or broken bones. Grabbed her purse, went into the kitchen, picked up her phone, and texted Auntie Jewel. Fell into a chair. Shut her eyes.

Cone of silence.

Spider looked at Jude like, *Are we in trouble or not?* Jude wondered if he should get his mother a beer from the fridge. He wondered if he should put a pizza in the microwave. Maybe if he acted like everything was okay . . .

"I drove all over town looking for you." Her eyes were still shut and her voice was flat as a run-over squirrel. "Everywhere, even across the tracks. I called the library, Jabari, every last freaking place I could think of. I called Jewel. She and Hal were out looking, too. Even Mr. Peters knows."

"I can explain."

"No." She opened her eyes. "No you cannot. Do not even try."

Suddenly, all he felt was tired. He'd never been this tired in his whole life.

"They gave me my notice today. Just like that." Mom tried to snap her fingers but they didn't make a sound. She rested her arms on the table and he saw how the edges of her uniform were frayed from all the times she'd washed it. It took a moment to process what she'd said.

"You mean, you got fired?"

"They don't call it fired. The snakes. The weasels. The two-faced, double-crossing, crap-eating cowards. They tell you your employment has been appreciated but as soon as you finish dinner service you are terminated. Please clean out your locker ASAP. Oh, and good luck."

He remembered Gladys saying how she hated when people misused language. They'd done the same thing to her father when he got fired.

"That's not right," he said. "That's not fair."

"That's what Miss Edith said when I told her. Poor Miss Edith. What's she going to do with all those doilies now?" His mother's laugh was small and hard. "She had a fit. That's not fair, she said. You're the best worker they've got. I told her, Miss Edith, no offense, but by your age you should know. Life is just like a dog. Give it a chance and it will bite."

Spider walked the T. rex up her arm. She swatted it away.

"They had the nerve to say they'd give me a good recommendation. Like jobs grow on trees around here? I told them just where they could shove their recommendation."

The words were angry, but her voice was worn out as her ugly uniform. Her job was hard—*hard*—but she'd done it. Every day, any shift they gave her, Mom showed up and did her best. How could they treat her like this? Jude wished she'd call Auntie Jewel who'd say I told you so and then they'd have an argument. He wished she'd go outside and holler at Mr. Peters about his light. He wished she'd do anything normal.

Then she did.

"So I came home. And what'd I find? What'd I find, Jude? You tell me."

"Mom, I'm sorry."

"No you're not. If you were really sorry, you'd quit letting me down like this. Driving home, I told myself, I still got my boys.

Nothing and nobody can take my two boys away from me. I walk in the door, and what do I find?"

"Mom—"

"I find you're gone. I find I can't trust you. Again. After last time I was sure you learned a lesson, but I was wrong. I swear, Jude. I don't even want to know where you were or what you thought was more important than your family. I don't care. It doesn't matter to me. You know what's worst of all?"

She paused like she really meant him to answer, but he knew better.

"You're teaching your little brother to lie. Lie and go behind my back. You know he looks up to you." Mom pushed back her chair. "I've been sitting here asking myself, what's left? What's still good? And I am coming up empty."

She picked up her phone and went down the hall. Jude followed her. Mr. Peters's light blazed through her bedroom window, flooding it with brightness. Then, just like that, it winked out. For a second, Mom and Jude stood there in darkness so sudden and total, it was like all the light in the world was gone.

Then Mom shut the door on him. She didn't come out the rest of the night.

☼

Gladys

Once, when Gladys was five or six and Dada still worked at the auto plant, they went to a Fourth of July barbecue at the home of a co-worker. The house was across the river, and it had a deck and a big backyard. Gladys wore a new outfit, red, white, and blue with sparkly stars (Mama still picked out her clothes then). Most of the kids were older than she was, and when it got dark they started a game of hide-and-seek. Gladys had played before, but never in a strange place, and never in the dark. When it came her turn to be it, she covered her eyes, nervously counted to one hundred, and spun around. Every single kid had disappeared.

In that instant, Gladys was convinced the other kids weren't just hiding: they'd vanished. She wasn't just alone. She'd been left behind, the only one. When she tried to move, she couldn't. When she tried to call *Ready or not*, fear stole her voice. Gladys began to cry and somehow, who knew how, all the way across the wide ocean of dark, up on the deck, Mama heard her. She came running, but Gladys was crying so hard she threw up and they had to go home.

Tonight, as Gladys got ready for bed, she tried not to think of True all alone in a place she'd never been.

But Gladys was no good at *not* thinking about things.

As she changed into her PJs, the mitten leaf drifted out of her overall pocket and onto the floor. She picked it up and sniffed it, the way True would. It had a fizzy smell, almost like root beer. Pinching it between two fingers, she went to her window and pushed back the curtains. The wind tossed the branches of the tree lawn tree. Clouds blotted out the stars. Did True understand that Gladys and Jude were trying to help, not hurt her? Could she understand that she hadn't been abandoned? That Gladys would be there as soon as she could?

"We're still here!" she called into the darkness. "You're not alone!"

"Glad?" Dada poked his head around her bedroom door. "Everything okay?"

"Oh! Umm." She set the leaf on her dictionary and sprang into bed. "Everything's fine!"

"Can I tuck you in?"

"That's okay. I'm going to read for a while." She picked up the summer reading book from her nightstand, even though she'd already finished it. "Actually, I'm getting kind of old for you and Mama to tuck me in."

He scratched his terrible beard. "How old are you?"

"Dada! You know I'm eleven!"

"Cannot be! Does not compute. System error. Please review data."

He did his robot-powering-down imitation, which always made her laugh, no matter what. She thought he'd go then, but he lingered, closing her curtains, picking some socks off the floor and rolling them together though they didn't match. Could he tell she was keeping secrets? Was he trying to give her the chance to confide in him? When he scratched his beard a few more times, kissed her forehead, took her old favorite toy, a bunny, off the shelf and kissed her, too, wished Gladys sweet dreams, and went out, gently closing the door behind him, Gladys had to stop herself from calling after him. *There* is *something*, she'd say. *Something I really need to tell you.*

But how could she? Her parents would make her take True back to her owner, a thought too horrible to contemplate. Gladys loved them, loved them with all her heart but not really, not *all* her heart, because now there were pieces she was keeping to herself, secret, troubling, maybe even dangerous pieces, and this made her sad and worried and even angry, but she couldn't help it. She couldn't help that she was changing into someone else. That she'd already changed. It wasn't her fault, was it?

But what if it was?

And what if Mama and Dada discovered that she wasn't the child they thought they'd adopted after all? Instead, they had a daughter who did things that would shock them. They might begin to think, *We made a big mistake.*

People could stop loving you. Gladys knew this very well.

She pulled the covers over her head. She could hear Jude saying, with what could only be termed a *sneer*, *Like everything's going to be okay because we* care? He made the word sound devious, like *unallocate* or *put to sleep*.

Gladys threw the covers back off and went to her dictionary. She turned the crinkly pages till she found *care*. Its many definitions took up almost a full page. *Care* was a noun, it was a verb. It meant something to worry about, it meant helping someone else. It could mean a wish or desire, it could mean to pay close attention. *Care* was one of those words like *star* or *dog* or *tree*—much too short and humble for all it represented.

Using the mitten leaf for a bookmark, she closed the dictionary, then set the alarm on her phone, laid out an outfit, turned off the light, and slipped back into bed. Pulling the covers over her head again, she listened to the rain begin to fall.

Jude

In the morning, it was raining hard. Mom stayed in bed. Sleeping in was something she always wished she could do, only now she wasn't sleeping. She was staring. When Mom put her mind to it, her eyes could bore holes in concrete.

"Mom?"

"Leave me be."

Ten minutes later, he tried again.

"Mom? You want something to eat?"

"Feed your brother."

He fixed Spider some cereal, then brought her a Coke. At last she sat up. Her hair was stuck to one side of her head and her eye makeup was smeared all around. The rain was really coming down.

He started worrying about True. But that sent his brain into overload.

Mom. He had to think about Mom.

Standing next to her bed, Jude felt too big. People thought being tall and strong was every guy's dream come true. Jabari said he'd sell his own sweet grandmother to be built like Jude. Towering over everybody, able to crush whoever bothered you like a bug beneath your shoe.

What people didn't get was, sometimes being big felt all wrong. It felt...fake. Like one of those words Gladys hated, words that covered up the real truth. Inside, you weren't big at all. You weren't anywhere near so strong as you looked.

When Jude was little, he had an action figure he loved. Army Man. Jude took that toy everywhere, except when Mom made him leave it home. He remembered being scared that while he was away, Army Man would disappear. Somebody would break in and steal him and when Jude got home, he'd be gone. Thinking that could make Jude cry, but he wouldn't tell Mom why. He wouldn't tell her that sometimes, when he was at daycare, he got scared she'd disappear, too. He'd wait and wait and she wouldn't come pick him up.

He knew she'd get mad if he told her that.

Now he stood by her bed, shifting from foot to foot. His mother was tall, too, but it seemed like she'd shrunk overnight. She set the Coke on her bedside table, then leaned back into her pillows. Mom was the queen of pillows. Her bed was heaped with them. Today, instead of luxurious, they looked like they might smother her.

"Get my purse," she said. "On the dresser."

When he brought it, she opened it and tossed out a new bunch of doilies. Found her wallet, pulled out a twenty.

"Take your brother to the Dollar Store and get yourselves a treat."

She never gave him money for no reason. Even when there was a reason, she almost never did. With the window shut, the air in the room was so stuffy, Jude had trouble pulling a breath.

"Shouldn't we be saving our money now?" he asked.

"Are you talking back to me?"

Jude had never in his life felt bad taking money, till now. He stuffed the bill in the pocket of his jeans.

"I'll buy school supplies," he said.

"I said a *treat*."

"Mom, come on!"

Like she didn't talk about money all the time. Like she hadn't said twelve million times, *This job doesn't pay enough for a bug to live on.* Like they weren't behind on the rent again, like their car wasn't a piece of junk, like if it wasn't for Auntie Jewel...

"Wipe that hangdog look off your face before I do it for you."

A small surge of hope. This sounded more like his real mother.

"People can knock you down, mister, but it's your own fault if you don't get back up. You stay down, you've got nobody to blame but your own sorry self."

He wanted to ask her how. Where was the money going to come from now? Auntie Jewel would help them in a heartbeat, but he knew better than to say that. It'd only make Mom madder. Or even worse, make her turn her face back to the wall.

"I can help," he said. "I can find a job after school."

"Your job is to turn things around in school this year. How many times do I have to tell you? I want you going to college. I want you succeeding."

"Yeah but meanwhile—"

"Forget meanwhile. We're going to be all right, Jude. Leave it to me. Now shut those blinds. This rain is getting on my last nerve."

He shut them and the room went twilight.

"Get Spy something he can't break in five minutes. Bring back any change and I'll bust your butt."

Jude zipped Spider into a jacket. He hunted up his brother's shoes and wedged his feet inside. They were getting too small.

Would she be mad if he spent the money on new sneakers? He went back to her room to say they were leaving.

She'd turned toward the wall. Hot as the room was, she had the covers up, but he could see her shoulders shaking. Mom hated to cry. The last time he could remember was when his father died. He remembered how she'd picked him up and crushed him against her so hard, it was like her crying was inside his own chest.

As he looked at her now, it happened again. Her hurt was inside him, too, ripping him up.

He didn't know how to stop it. He didn't know how to help.

Gladys

Jude needs my help. Will be home by supper if not sooner. Yes I have my phone and will wear my helmet.

   Your loving daughter, Gladys

She'd gotten up extra early and left the note on the kitchen table, then slipped out the back door. She hoped Mama would understand, possibly even approve of, helping Jude.

Even if it wasn't exactly, precisely, exclusively Jude she needed to help.

Outside the wind laughed at her puny bike. *Ha ha!* it sneered, trying to knock her over. The dumb flag on the back flapped as if it was having a panic attack. The rain was cold, an end-of-summer rain she hadn't dressed for. She accidentally sped through a big puddle, soaking her espadrilles and spattering her capris.

When she got to the tracks she stopped, even though there wasn't a train in sight.

Every kid in town had gotten the lecture about the other side of the tracks. Parents read the riot act on the numerous dangers of playing there: broken glass, rusty nails, moldy walls, rats and bats and unsavory people. One of whom was found frozen solid in a basement last winter.

Blood beating up in her ears, she pushed off and pedaled across the tracks.

It was hard to see with the rain, but Jude's directions were good. She passed a few houses with lights on, like lonely outposts on the frontier. The street he described had an abandoned red house on the corner, then an empty field, and then another house, this one with a pointy roof and a half-dead tree out front. She'd told Sophie that houses couldn't see or hear, but now she wondered if they could have souls. *Forsaken*, that was the word for this place. If she didn't know True was here, she'd turn around, speed home, and dive back into bed.

She walked her bike partway up the driveway, then stopped. The wind bent the tall grass and made the tree branches creak. Water trickled under the collar of her shirt and her toes curled inside her wet shoes. There were probably bats in that house, furry, possibly rabid bats hanging upside down from the rafters. Gladys had an irrational fear of bats. Irrational fears were more powerful than rational ones. Though she had plenty of rational fears right now, too.

She needed to focus.

She tiptoed up the back steps and inside. In the dismal kitchen, someone named TED had crayoned his name on the wall, giving the E extra lines, just like Sophie did. A beat-up broom leaned in one corner. Beneath a table were two familiar pans, both overturned.

"True?" she squeaked. "Are you here?"

Rain on the roof was the only sound.

Gladys stepped into the hallway, directly into a pile of poop. "Yuck!"

As she tried to scrape it off her shoe, the stink blended with the other noxious smells of mildew and rot. The window at the end of the hallway was so dirty, and the rain was coming down so hard, almost no light got through. Behind her, something batted the air. She spun around in time to glimpse a vanishing shadow.

Batted. No. Please no.

What was that faint scrabbling noise? Bats didn't scrabble, did they? Rats, though. Rats scrabbled. Also people high on drugs.

The floorboards groaned, making her jump before she realized it was her own feet that had done it. She pressed herself against the wall, wishing Jude was here. He was so big. Although Gladys tried never to use being small as an excuse for anything, there were times—times such as right this minute—when she urgently wished she was much bigger and stronger.

Someone whimpered. Possibly her.

Halfway down the hall, a door stood partly open. Trying not to breathe, Gladys nudged it with her foot. Another nudge, and then she peeked around it.

It was a bathroom, with an old-fashioned bathtub, the kind with feet that looked like claws. Wedged underneath . . .

"You're here!" Gladys crouched beside her. "I was so worried."

True's ears went flat. She looked confused and then, as if she was sorry but she couldn't help herself, she bared her teeth, just the way she had behind Freddy's. Gladys scooched back, wrapping her arms around herself.

"All right. I know it's been a long scary night. I mean, a long scary forever. I'm so sorry. I got here as soon as I could. Are you hungry?"

Stepping carefully over the poop pile, she retrieved a pan from the kitchen, poured in the kibble—how could the bag already be half empty?—stepped back over the poop, and carried the pan to the bathroom, where she set it on the floor beside the tub. She was careful to keep her hands to herself, which was doubly hard since, huddled in her bathtub cave, True looked more huggable than ever.

"Breakfast!" Gladys said softly. "Come and get it!"

True eyed the food hungrily but didn't move.

"Don't be stubborn! I know you like it. You already ate half the bag!"

But when she inched closer, the dog growled and Gladys shrank back, a tiny bit frightened but mostly disappointed. And hurt. She'd hardly slept all night, worrying, and she'd expected True to be as overjoyed to see her as she was to see True.

Clearly she didn't know everything.

As certain people had pointed out to her.

Gladys slid down onto the floor. She'd brought soap, a towel, and an old comb she'd found in a bathroom drawer. She'd planned to clean True up, but that wasn't going to happen. Her phone pinged with a text from Mama.

What are you and Jude up to?

Who'd have guessed this decrepit place had cell reception? A second later, another text.

And where?

Where was she? Someplace she'd never been. Someplace where, not very long ago, she'd have been astonished to find herself. Someplace she definitely could not reveal to her mother, who'd jump in the car and speed directly here.

Just hanging out. She hesitated, hating to lie to Mama. *At the house*, she added, and hit send. Guilt washing over her, she quickly texted Jude.

Found her!

The bathroom's only window was set high in the wall and its glass was murky green. Hunched on the floor, cold and wet, Gladys tried not to notice the spiderwebs in every corner, or the stink of unidentified, rotting objects, not to mention the stink of her own poopy espadrille. She tried not to think about a bat getting tangled in her hair, and she tried not to notice the skittering, scratching sounds in the walls, and she especially tried not to imagine a dead body in the basement. She gave Jude another minute, then texted again.

We need more dog food!!

Still no answer. She tried not to think how she'd lied to Mama, how she'd need to keep on lying. She tried not to think about all the possible reasons Jude wasn't answering her.

When it came to not thinking, Gladys really was an abject failure.

Hello? she texted. *U there?*

True's head poked out from under the tub. Pyramid ears,

the left one with a notch, shaggy eyebrows, summer-sky eyes. As she angled herself toward the door, her sweet face settled into that familiar, patient, hopeful expression. She rested her head on her paws, waiting.

Who? Who was she waiting for? The bad boyfriend, that guy with the motorcycle? Mrs. Marsh said he used to play with True in the yard. Maybe he'd loved True. But if he really had, wouldn't he have taken her with him when he left? It'd be difficult, on a motorcycle, but if he loved her enough, he could've figured it out. Instead he'd roared off and left her in his dust. With a woman who despised her. True didn't understand. She'd given him her heart, as trusting as a baby, and now she just kept waiting.

"He gave you up," Gladys said. "I'm sorry, but it doesn't look like he's coming back."

The rain was gentler now. It tapped softly on the window, and Gladys could hear True's quiet breathing. In out, in out, her eyes on the empty doorway.

"It's okay to let your sad out. Go ahead. It's a mistake to bottle up your true feelings, the way Jude does."

When Gladys said his name, True's left ear twitched. She swiveled her head to fix Gladys with a hopeful, expectant look.

"Jude," Gladys said again, testing. This time both ears pricked upright. "Jude?" Her tail swept the floor.

Gladys swallowed.

"He's not here," she said. "But I am! And I always will be. You can depend on me. Looking for you was all my idea, you know. I had to practically force him. Not that you can actually force Jude to do anything."

A soft, inquisitive whine. *Jude?*

"I don't know where he is. Anyway, *my* name is Gladys. *Gladys.*"

With an apologetic sigh, True turned back toward the door.

Gladys leaned against the wall.

It wasn't the motorcycle guy True was waiting for. Maybe it used to be, but not anymore.

It wasn't Gladys either.

"True," she called softly. "True?"

Reluctantly, the dog turned to look at her. Wordless communication flew between them.

It's him, isn't it? Gladys.

He'll come, won't he? True.

The little cave opened inside her. Dark and cold, it was a place with no words. A place before words, where fierce feelings prowled around, thudding into each other, scaring and confusing her. Gazing into True's troubled eyes, Gladys knew the dog had an emptiness inside, too, a wordless place aching to be filled with light and warmth.

What good were words and definitions after all? Gladys had them now, thousands upon thousands of them, but here she was, helpless to name what was inside her. All she could do was reach out, slowly and gently, to touch the top of True's head the way Jude did. Like Jude, she ran her hand slowly and deliberately along the matted, dirty fur, trying to calm whatever was going on inside that bony rib cage, trying to speak with her heart.

Gladys picked up her phone, hesitated a long moment, then texted him again.

True needs u I can tell

This time, he answered right away.

How?
How what?
Can u tell?
I see it in her eyes
She waited, but there was no answer.

Jude

Their sorry umbrella was no match for the wind. Jude shoved it into the first trash can they passed. Spider whined his head off and for once Jude couldn't blame him. The Dollar Store was on the very edge of town, and by the time they got there, they were drowned rats. The BACK TO SCHOOL stuff took up a whole depressing aisle. Spider hung a left, headed for the toys. Jude started to follow him, but his phone pinged with a text.

Found her!

Jude exhaled. He hadn't realized how worried he was that she'd flake. Yeah, she'd *said* she'd go, and yeah, she was stubborn as dirt, but still. Kids bigger than her would've been scared to go to the house alone. Not to mention, it was a monsoon out there.

It was probably time to quit being surprised by this girl.

His thumbs twitched. He had a million questions. Was True okay? Had she been howling and barking? Had Gladys seen anybody else on the street? How long could she stay? Did she come up with a better plan yet?

Ping!

We need more dog food!!

Spider was pulling toys off the shelf and lining them up on the floor for inspection. An old lady in a plastic rain hat carefully stepped around him.

Ping!

Hello? U there?

The girl had lightning fingers.

"This!" announced Spider, choosing a plastic train set. "And this." A box of plastic dinosaurs. He started for the checkout, leaving the mess of toys all over the floor.

"Hey kid!" called the guy at the checkout. "This your brother?"

Spider had cut to the head of the line and was putting his stuff on the counter

Ping!

True needs u I can tell

He stared at the phone.

"Coming!" Jude started throwing the toys back on the shelf with one hand, texting with the other.

How?

How what?

Can u tell?

A pause. Jude stood up and stared at his phone, willing her to answer.

Ping!

I see it in her eyes

Gladys

Gladys folded her arms on her knees and rested her head. Which was so heavy, it felt like a sack of rocks attached to her neck. It felt as if it was someone else's head, laden with someone else's thoughts, wrongly attached to her body. Jude hadn't answered her last text. What if he ditched her and True? What if he was right, and caring wasn't enough? What if . . .

Her head was so heavy.

True growled and Gladys jerked awake. The room was brighter, the greenish window glowing. She'd drifted off, and now someone was in the house. True's ears were pricked and the fur on her back stood up in that wolf-like ridge. The floorboards creaked, then went silent. Gladys scooted backward, wedging herself between the tub and wall, hoping somebody high on drugs would miss seeing her. The floorboards creaked, went silent.

"Gladys?"

She leaped up, banged her knee against the tub, and face-planted. When she tried to get up, her toe caught in a crack in the floorboards and she tumbled over sideways. True barked a joyful bark Gladys had never heard before as Jude asked them, "Are you guys okay?"

He was slick with rain or sweat or both. His cheeks were

pink as bubble gum. True jumped up, doing her funny little dance. Setting her paws on Jude's knees, she tried to lick his face but had to settle for his hands and arms.

"Whoa, ugh!" he said, pretending to be grossed out while grinning like a lunatic. "Hey, quit the slobber!"

The two of them were so happy—no, *ecstatic*. It was the kind of happiness that brims and spills over onto everything and everyone in the vicinity, showering them with joy so that, for one whole second, possibly even longer, Gladys forgot to be jealous. But then she remembered.

"This place feels sinister," she said, but he ignored her.

"Luckily there's some big end-of-summer thing going on at the library. I left Spy there." He was reaching into a Dollar Store bag. "I brought you a treat," he told True, holding up a rawhide bone. "I got more food, too," he told Gladys.

And then he smiled at her.

His true, sun-breaking-through-the-clouds smile.

Jude

The rain had stopped and the world shone like a car rolling out of Ultimate Car Wash. Jude grinned, picturing a giant with a massive cloth shining up the grass and sky. Pookie was so glad to be back out in the yard, she ran around in circles, then sprinted straight-out full speed, zapping the rope from his hand. Just before she hit the garage she did a backpedal right out of a cartoon, reversed, and ran back to where they stood.

Then she did it again.

And again.

"That is what you call pure joy," Gladys said.

"Joy?" He couldn't resist. "You don't got a bigger word?"

"It *is* a big word," she said, all serious.

Pookie wore herself out and flopped down in the grass. Panting. Grinning. When Jude gave her the chew-bone, she took it between her paws and went to town.

Like an engine. Like an engine that sputtered out, but always started up again. An engine of joy, that's what a dog was.

"Where's the fortress?" Gladys asked.

This girl had a warped sense of humor.

He crossed the yard to the entrance and bowed like some butler-dude.

Her too-big eyes went even bigger. She hesitated a second, then ducked—she hardly even had to duck—inside.

"You built this?"

"Me and Jabari."

"Umm, wow."

"I know." He wanted to crawl in beside her, but that'd be too close for comfort. "It's even better at night."

"It's scary enough in broad daylight."

He watched Pookie chew her bone like an ordinary, happy, un-whacked-out dog.

"Speaking of scary." He cleared his throat. "My mom got laid off yesterday."

"No! Really? I can't believe it!" She poked her head back out, looking furious. Like she actually couldn't believe it, like his mother was the first person this had ever happened to. Like the same thing hadn't happened to her father and half the people in town by now.

Jude appreciated this.

"My mother says life's like a dog. If it can bite, it will."

"Not True though."

Did she mean it wasn't true, or that True wouldn't bite?

"Anyway, I'm really, sincerely sorry about your mom," she said. "When my father lost his job at the plant, he took it hard. I mean, he's still taking it hard. Even though he pretends he's okay, I can tell." She pinched the plastic on the Beautyrest. "He's hoping Crooked River will make him permanent, but there's no telling."

"It's not his fault."

"I know. But still." She pinched the plastic again, then folded her hands. "When you're small, when you're still a sprout, you think your parents have superpowers. You believe they know everything! Can fix anything! Maybe you have to feel that way, since you need them so much. If you didn't believe it, life would be too scary."

He was listening.

"Then you get older and you start to understand that they can't do everything, no matter how hard they try. Sometimes they make mistakes. They might even make mistakes about you. Big mistakes! They're really not all-powerful. It's confusing. Also...kind of scary."

That was the third time she'd said *scary*.

"Sad, too," he heard himself say, and she nodded.

"Remember how when you're little, you couldn't wait to be big? Me, obviously I'm still waiting to be big on the outside, but anyway, I'm talking about the inside. When you're a sprout you think growing up is going to be the best thing. Your life will just keep getting better and better." She fingered the tips of her weird little scarf. "Then one day, everything gets complicated. All of a sudden it's like you're looking into one of those three-way mirrors they have in stores. You see parts of yourself that you never did before. Still, there they are. And they are you, whether you like it or not."

She stopped talking, like she really wanted to hear what he thought. He was pretty sure she was biting her tongue, making herself wait.

"But you love them, right?" he asked.

"Who?"

"Your parents."

"My parents? That's a bizarre question."

"It's just...I'm not trying to be rude, okay? But I never knew anybody who was adopted."

"Oh." She looked away. "I didn't mean to tell you that, actually. It came out accidentally."

He was surprised how much it hurt him to hear her say that.

"Anyway," he said. "Never mind. Your parents seem cool."

Eye-roll. "I guess you didn't notice my father's beard." Then, just like that, her face crumpled.

What? Her father's beard was bad, but not that bad. He looked at Pookie, chomping her bone, and he suddenly wondered if dogs missed their mothers. He hoped not.

"Do you ever feel like you're not sure who you're supposed to be?" she asked then.

"No. I know who I'm supposed to be. It's just, I can't always be him."

How'd she get him to say that? He hadn't even known he was thinking it. Listening to her talk so much, something inside him came loose. She undid knots.

"You know what I hate?" he heard himself say next. "How adults tell you life's not fair, so you better get used to it. Next second, they do a 180. They say, you can be whatever you want to be. Just follow your dream and it'll come true. Like, what? How can those both be true?"

She nodded hard, her hair waving around. "I'm convinced most adults don't listen to half of what they say."

"Then why do they even say it? Why don't they just shut up?"

"It's a good question." She looked at her phone. "You've been here an hour. You better go get Spy. He's probably tearing up the library by now." She ducked out of the fortress. "Just wait one minute."

Jude pulled the tarp back in place. When he and Pook went inside the house, he saw that she'd cleaned up the poop pile. She'd used an old towel to make a dog bed on the bathroom floor. Her little scarf, printed with boats and anchors, was spread across it. Who knew how she'd reached that high-up window and opened it to let in fresh air? By now she was back in full know-it-all, boss-of-the-universe mode.

"Before you go," she said, "you have to leave something with your scent on it, to reassure her that you'll be back." She pointed at his pocket. "How about that book you're always carrying?" When he pulled it out, her eyes went round. "I wondered what that book was. I would've guessed a hundred other things before a tree guide."

"Yeah well. Trees are interesting."

"I agree." She nodded. "There is no synonym for *tree*."

He hated to leave it behind, but if it'd help Pookie? When he set the book on the dog nest they both laughed. It looked like bedtime reading.

He was going to have to run most of the way to the library.

But he hated to go. Every time he left her, it was harder.

Gladys

How's Jude?" Mama asked when Gladys got home.

The fortress! It was a collection of junk, tetanus waiting to happen. When Jude ushered her in, she'd thought he was pranking her. Inside was a little better but still, basically, just a bunch of stuff nobody wanted anymore, arranged into a flimsy shelter. It took a fertile imagination to see it as a fortress, to turn something so random into something powerful and protective.

He'd trusted her to see it that way, too.

The book he carried everywhere was a guide to *trees*.

He'd had a long, serious conversation with her.

Jude was not what he first seemed. Gladys had suspected it all along, but now she knew for sure.

He'd let her inside his secret fortress. She had the feeling he was surprised he'd done that.

"Gladys," Mama said, more sternly. "Is Jude okay?"

He and True had been so happy to see each other! After Jude left for the library, True had curled up in her doggy bed, sniffed the tree book, and gone fast asleep, serene and secure. Gladys was still jealous, but not so much. Instead, she began to feel uneasy.

"Please answer me," Mama said.

"He's okay." Her mother looked dubious, so Gladys added, "Actually, he's probably the happiest I've ever seen him."

"Ah." Mama leaned back. "I knew it. You're the good friend he needed." She wrinkled her nose. "When's the last time you took a shower, sugar? You smell a little musty."

Jude

Jude picked up Spider from the library and hustled him home. Auntie Jewel was in the kitchen, heating a pot of her homemade chili. She gave him and Spider big, perfumey hugs, then served them heaping bowls. While they ate, she tried to repair the Dollar Store train set Spider had already broken.

"Your mother's been like this since last night?" she asked.

"Pretty much."

"Good Sam!" Auntie scowled. "There's nothing good about that place! They worked her to the bone then kicked her to the curb. I told her this would happen! She should've quit and come work for me and Hal long ago."

"Don't blame her," Jude said. "She tried her best. And blame doesn't help anything."

She looked at him. Set the train down and puffed a breath. "This toy is a piece of junk, baby." She heaped another bowl with chili, got a can of Mountain Dew, and went down the hall to Mom's room.

Jude started counting. He was only up to eight when the arguing started.

• • •

That night Jude stood in the backyard and texted Gladys.

Hope shes not barking & howling

Me too

Now that Mr. Peters had killed the security light, it was black as the bottom of a well out here. Something moved in the old guy's yard. Was it a skunk? Jude took a step back.

U? Gladys texted.

I dont bark or howl

Funny. Meant r u ok? And your mom?

Jude could see Mr. Peters at his kitchen table. He had a napkin tucked into his shirt collar. He was eating something with a spoon and watching a little TV set on the counter. When you saw Mr. Peters outside, he looked like he had a whole life going on. But inside, he looked lonesome as an orphan.

Jude felt embarrassed and turned away. Instead of answering her question, he texted *C u tomorrow*

There was a long pause, like she was hoping for more. Then, *K*

Gladys

To her surprise, the next morning Gladys found Dada, wearing normal clothes, drinking coffee alone in the kitchen.

"My establishment has graciously granted me a day of leisure." He poured her a cup, half cream. "Translation: my hours got cut."

Dada had told Mama to take the chance to sleep in. No sprouts had arrived yet, and the house was quiet. It was so rare, so nice. Gladys could tell that her father wanted her to sit with him, sipping their coffees, eating the muffins he'd baked, just the two of them together. A part of her murmured it wanted the exact same thing, but another part, a more vociferous part, pointed out that this was her chance to get away. Maybe Dada could hear that voice, too. Before long, he stretched, scratched his beard, and said didn't she have anything better to do than sit around here on her day off?

Gladys hugged him and ran out the door. Then ran back in and hugged him again.

When she got to the fortress house, a man stood out front.

"What do you think you're doing here, little girl?" He wore a dirty sweatshirt and had long greasy hair. Gladys froze.

"Uh," she said. "Just . . . just riding my bike."

"This ain't no place for a young girl. There's junkies. There's vermin. There's wild dogs."

"Dogs?"

"I live down the road." He pointed to the red house on the corner, which she'd been sure was unoccupied. "I hear them at night, barking and howling. Dogs is pack animals, like wolves. You want to get bit? You want to get rabies?"

"No!"

"Then git on home to your mama."

Gladys rode all the way back to the tracks, where she texted Jude. At last he came jogging and panting toward her.

"Auntie Jewel took Spy for the day. I told my mom I was going to tutoring at the library, then staying to do my summer reading. I really did bring the stupid book." He held up a paperback, as if for proof, then lowered it slowly. "What's wrong? Is Pook okay?"

When she told him about the man, he cursed under his breath.

"I was afraid she'd bark," he said, "but I hoped nobody'd hear her. Well, come on. She's hungry by now."

"But what if that guy sees me again? He'll get suspicious."

"I'll tell him you're my little sister and you got no sense and I came to take you home."

"What? Like I'm *Spider*?"

"You coming or not?"

Nobody was in sight as they slipped up the driveway and inside the house, where True Blue waited directly inside the kitchen door. They took her out in the yard where she did her business, and then they filled her pans and watched her eat and drink. Dog care, Gladys was realizing, had a lot in common with childcare. Food, poop, pee, sleep, repeat. Jude filled a Super Soaker lying in the grass and shot arcs of water, rainbows sparkling in the sun. True leaped up, trying to catch them again and again. Jude laughed, but the uneasiness Gladys had started to feel only got worse.

"We should go in," she said. "In case that man comes snooping around again."

"One more minute," said Jude.

More like twenty, but at last, carrying her pans, they went back inside, where True lapped up her water, trotted into the bathroom, circled her bed three times, and lay down with a paw on the tree book. She looked up from under her shaggy brows, eyes shining for one brief moment before they closed and she began to softly, sweetly snore. Jude laughed.

"What's so funny?" Gladys asked, and he shrugged.

"She reminds me of somebody, the way she snores." He sat down next to True. "My mom, if you gotta know."

Gladys watched him ease the tree book out from under True's paw and leaf through the pages. *Leaf*—that was funny, considering.

"I hardly know anything about trees," she said.

"You got a nice sycamore in your backyard."

"Are you going to be an arborist when you grow up?"

"Huh?" He didn't try to hide his smile. His luminous smile! "What are you even talking about now?"

She perched on the edge of the tub, which was highly uncomfortable, so she stood back up. It was such a cozy scene. Why did she feel anxious?

"Shouldn't you be reading your book for school?"

"Give me a break!"

"I mean, school starts soon."

"Wow. News flash."

"We'll be there all day."

"Don't remind me."

"We'll have to leave True alone even more than we do now."

"So?" He frowned, bending his head over his book. "Lots of dogs are by themselves all day."

"All night, too," she said.

He turned a page. Gladys thought of her dictionary, how just turning its whispery pages could make her feel better.

"We *rescued* her," he said. "You said so yourself."

"I know, but . . ."

"And you didn't have a plan, so we brought her here and guess what? It's working out okay. She likes it here."

"I know. It's just I'm not sure—"

"Wait." He slapped the book shut. "Did you go back to that house? Did you see her again?"

"No! I don't ever want to go back there."

"Then don't. There's no reason to go."

"Do you have to get so angry? I'm just—"

"That fossil! She didn't deserve Pook."

"I know! You're absolutely right."

"So?" he said again. True had started to whimper, the way she did when they argued, and he rubbed under her chin. "So what's the problem then?" he asked, voice soft.

The man down the street. The coming cold weather and a house with no heat. The price of dog food. How in the world she could go on keeping this a secret from Mama and Dada.

Those were problems.

But how could she say that? She couldn't, not when Jude began to stroke True the way she liked, from the top

184

of her head down her shaggy back, and True's crooked tail thumped, and she snuggled even deeper into her bed. Not after promising that, if only they cared enough, everything would be okay.

She had to figure out a way to make this work.

Jude

As he headed for his front door, something caught his eye. His white pine.

A green shoot.

The tree was growing again! Like, *Think you can kill me? Think again.* Like, *Dude, did you really believe I'd give up?*

Like, *I forgive you.*

Could trees come back from the dead? Jude's hand went to his pocket before he remembered he'd given Pook his book. The afternoon sun made the tip of the branch shine like a green star. He whipped out his phone, took a picture.

Some moments you wanted to stretch out as long as possible. He could still feel Pookie's head warm on his knee, still see her looking at him like she knew exactly who he was, and who he was was exactly right.

What if his pine tree was a sign? Like Mom said. People can knock you down, but it's your own fault if you don't get back up.

Maybe it was a signal. Things could turn around. Things were going to work out.

He sent the photo to Gladys. Lightning Fingers texted right back.

Verdant

That girl. What did she even mean? Smiling, he opened the door and went in.

"Mom? Mom, I'm home!"

Gladys

Each time she looked at the photo Jude sent, her foolish heart beat up with happiness. It was blurry, as if his hand shook when he snapped it. Something green, possibly a caterpillar? For a boy as miserly with his texts as his conversation, it was mysterious and wonderful.

Jude was acting as if they were friends. Not only that. He believed that True belonged to them now. She was theirs, and Jude was ready to do whatever it took to keep her.

Not long ago, either of those two things would have filled Gladys with happiness. Put together, they'd have practically made her delirious.

Be careful what you wish for, adults cautioned. Such dreary, depressing advice! But now Gladys understood that the two things she'd wished for—making Jude her friend and saving True—those two things were twined so tightly that if you pulled one loose, the other would fall away, too.

Keeping True at the fortress was supposed to be temporary, till they figured out what to do next. But Jude—and not just Jude but True too—had started thinking of it as forever. This was her fault. She'd told Jude that if he cared enough, things would work out. And now he did care, cared so much it would break his heart to give up True.

It would break her heart, too.

But what else could they do?

Maybe if she told Jude it wasn't fair to True. As long as they kept her, there was always the chance something would go wrong. Didn't True deserve a home she'd never have to worry about losing? A real home, with toys to play with, a dish always full of kibble, evening walks around the block on a real leash and then a soft bed to circle three times and sink into with a sweet doggy sigh, knowing she'd wake up tomorrow to another perfect doggy day.

What was more important: being safe or being with someone you loved?

Maybe that wasn't even the real question. Maybe the real question was why should anyone ever have to choose?

She and Sophie were waiting for Mrs. Myers. Sophie had worn her fairy costume today and was flitting around the front yard with her magic wand. The leaves of the tree lawn tree were turning the color of butter. What kind of tree was it? Gladys had never wondered before.

Sophie tapped her with the magic wand.

"I grant you one wish," she said.

"I wish you were a frog."

Sophie leaped around, croaking, but when her mother's pickup turned into the driveway, she immediately morphed back into a little girl, running with arms open wide as if she and her mother had been separated for years.

"Mommy! My best Mommy ever!"

"Sophie Marie!" Mrs. Myers swept her up. "My best darling girl! What do you say we go home?"

Gladys watched her buckle Sophie into her car seat, then climb behind the wheel.

"Thank you!" she called to Gladys as the truck clanked away.

What do you say we go home?

Home was one of those words. Four letters, that was all. Yet some people might say it was the most powerful word in the entire English language.

Maybe in any language.

Gladys went up to her room and sat on her bed. She opened her laptop and typed in *animal shelter.*

A gazillion hits.

She closed the lid and pulled a breath, trying to calm her skittering heart.

Jude

"You smell funny," Mom said. She was at the kitchen table, hunched over her laptop. She wrinkled her nose. "Funky. Like a dog."

"Ha!" Jude's face caught fire. "Yeah, well, they had a dog at the library. You can read to it." This was actually true. He'd seen kids do it. The dog slept the whole time but the kids still believed it was listening.

He thought of True and his tree book and smiled.

"Now I heard everything." Mom studied him. "How was tutoring?"

"Great. I mean, it was boring. But I learned stuff. And I got like halfway through the summer reading." He waved the book. Page three wasn't exactly halfway. Time to change the subject. "What are you doing?"

"Trying to figure out how to use the system optimizations to be a claimant for my initial UC."

"That makes zero sense."

She closed the laptop. Her skin was too white, like his, but now it also looked too thin. The scar on her lip looked too red.

"It makes as much sense as having a freaking dog in a library." She stood up. "I didn't sleep last night. I need to lie down."

"Mom." A hand was pressing down on his chest, squeezing

the air out. He tried to call back the hope he'd felt a few minutes ago, standing by his tree. "I...I want to do something. I can help."

"Keep going to that tutoring. That's helping."

"But I mean really helping."

"You *really* want to help? When my nosy sister brings Spy home, tell her I'm asleep and nobody but nobody better wake me up and give me a lecture on how to live my life."

She slumped down the hall, shut the door to her room.

He opened her laptop and typed in *jobs for 11 year olds*.

Babysitter was number one.

Number two was *pet sitter*.

Two jobs he already had.

For no money.

He shut the laptop and kicked the leg of the table.

Kicked it hard.

Gladys

The next day, after lunch, Mama took the obstreperous Mateo out in the backyard to keep him from disturbing the other sprouts. Gladys was the nap warden, sitting on the couch surrounded by cots.

She texted Jude to let him know she was stuck here, but he didn't answer. For the first time, his non-communicativeness was a relief. Gladys didn't really want to talk to him.

She'd found an animal shelter two towns away. The website said it was "no kill," straightforward language Gladys appreciated. She'd scrolled through dozens of photos of dogs and cats waiting for homes. Each one had a long, loving description of his or her personality and needs. Whoever wrote the descriptions was just like Mama, certain you'd find good if you only looked.

For Duke, patience and consistency are key!

Kuddles can be highly anxious, but with the right care she lives up to her name.

The shelter was strict about one thing: absolutely no dropping off animals. The owner had to bring the dog or cat in and fill out official papers in order to "surrender" it.

Surrender was a heart-crushing word.

Gladys got up from the couch and tiptoed to the kitchen, where she looked out the back door. Mateo was conked out on

Mama's shoulder, but she was still patiently walking up and down, up and down, beneath the tree that looked like a reptile shedding its skin. Which she now knew was a sycamore.

Mama and Dada had a zillion photos of the day they'd brought her home for good. She'd looked like a miniature Yoda, only with hair. Lots of hair. If someone had written a description of her, it would have said, *Gladys is very small for her age, with no guarantee she'll catch up. She rarely speaks and has nightmares every night. Gladys needs a very special couple to give her a forever home.*

Mama turned. How did she always know when Gladys was near? Their eyes met. Wordless communication flew between them.

Okay? Mama asked.

Gladys gave a thumbs-up, spun around, and ran back to the couch. where she texted Jude.

Everything ok?

Jude

Jude fixed his eyes on his sneakers, fooling with the laces, while he told Mom he was going back to tutoring. Lucky for him, Mom never went to the library, so she had no clue tutoring had ended two weeks ago.

He was sick of lying to her. But what was he supposed to do? Besides, his lying made her happy. It made her think at least one thing, namely him, was going right.

On Front Street, a few cars were parked outside the thrift shop, and Jake the barber sat in a chair on the sidewalk waiting for customers. Avoiding Freddy's, Jude checked shop windows, looking for a HELP WANTED sign. No luck. He headed toward the library. He'd stop in, so when he told Mom he'd been there, it wouldn't be a total...

Wait.

A sign stapled to a telephone pole. He stepped close to read it.

LOST DOG

A picture of a dog with a stripe down the middle of its face. The picture was black-and-white, and the dog's eyes were light gray. Its ears were up, and its mouth hung open in a smile that made Jude's heart jump. Some dude had his arm around the dog. The arm, covered with tattoos, was all you could see of him. The rest of the picture was torn away.

$500 REWARD NO QUESTIONS ASKED

Like a freight train roaring through his chest, that was how it felt. The edges of the sign curled like it had got rained on. He pulled it down and stuffed it in his pocket. Looked around to make sure no one had seen him. Jogged up the street, around the corner. Two more flyers. He tore those down, too, then searched some more, but couldn't find any others. How long had they been up? Had he missed them before?

He hustled to the old church where they'd taken Pookie the day they found her. Sitting at the picnic table, he examined the photo. This dog had meat on her bones. Her fur was clean and brushed. Jude squinted. Her left ear had a notch in it.

The freight train was sucking him in, pulling him under. Trying to calm down, he studied the leaves overhead. Sassafras trees had three kinds. An oval. A mitten. A shape like a chubby person with both arms raised. You really got your money's worth with a sassafras. If you were trying to sell one, you could advertise three trees in one. You could . . .

Jude took out his phone and called the number on the flyer. Two rings.

"Hello?"

It was her.

"Hello? Who is this?"

He ended the call, hand shaking. He was about to put his phone away when it chimed with a text.

Stuck home all day climbing the walls

Jude set the phone down without answering.

Five hundred dollars? The lady didn't look like she had that much money. But who knew? He'd heard about loony-tune people hiding fortunes under their mattresses or in their freezers and nobody knew till they died.

So it was possible.

Though why was she offering a reward at all? She didn't care about Pook. The opposite. She was all about *This dog is a massive pain in my butt*, not offering a mountain of money to get the dog back. And it wasn't like she'd posted a lot of signs.

Still, here it was in black-and-white.

What if he could get that money and give it to Mom?

Ping!

Everything ok?

He shoved the phone in his pocket.

By the time he neared the fortress, Jude's brain was chasing its own tail. When he saw someone standing out front, for a second he thought it was the guy who'd scared Gladys and he about freaked.

Then he realized it was Jabari.

Gladys

Was Jude at the fortress? Was True okay? Gladys leaned back on the couch, her worry growing. Usually, worry was a passing thing, like having the sniffles. Now it had taken over, like a terminal disease.

Much as she dreaded it, she needed to talk to him. She texted him again.

Why hadn't he answered?

What in the world was he doing?

Jude

They saw each other at the same time.

"Jabari."

"Jude Dude." Jabari rubbed his birthmark. "I wanted to make sure nobody was messing with our stuff."

"Thanks."

"The other day, some jacked-up guys stripped the plumbing from an empty house on my gram's street."

"That bites."

"So I came to check. You know, protect our territory."

Jude didn't ask what Jabari planned to do if some jacked-up guys tried to steal from here. He was too glad to be talking to his friend, too glad to hear him say *our territory* like he used to.

"Thanks," Jude said again. He cleared his throat. "Hey. I . . . what happened. I wish it didn't."

"Yeah. Me too." Jabari studied his shoes. They were new. School shoes. He looked up. "How's the Tarantula?"

Jude put his finger in his mouth, pretending to puke.

Jabari nodded. He waved a hand in front of his face like he was swatting away a fly, only there was no fly, and then he held up a fist and they were doing their old secret shake. Relief swept through Jude. Good old Jabari! *Good old Jabari.*

Jude had forgotten that when you first heard Pookie

barking, she sounded like a cross between a cement mixer and a wolf. So when she started in now, Jabari froze. His eyes bugged. His head swiveled toward the house.

"What the?" he said.

"There's this thing," Jude told him. "That happened."

· · ·

They sat in the fortress doorway, watching Pookie nose around in the backyard. Jude explained. And explained. It wore his mouth out, all that explaining.

When he got to the part about showing Gladys the fortress, he jumped up and paced back and forth. Jabari would be steamed and who could blame him? They'd sworn each other to secrecy. But when he dared a look at his friend, Jabari wore a funny expression. Like he knew something Jude didn't.

"What?"

"Your face. It's like a red water balloon. I think you got a fever."

"No I don't."

"Oh right. You don't got a fever. You got a *girlfriend*."

"I will mess you up!" Jude yelled, and then they were play-fighting just like they used to. They swung and kicked and dodged and chased, and it felt so good. Jabari had him in a fake choke hold when out of nowhere Pookie sank her teeth into Jabari's basketball shorts.

"No!" Jude shouted. "No, girl!"

Jabari started screaming. Pookie swung her head back and forth, holding on, snarling like she meant to make hamburger out of him.

"It's okay, Pook!" Jude told her. "Back off! Let go!"

She raced away barking, running around in a circle till she collapsed panting in the dirt by the garage.

Jabari leaped up the back steps, flattened himself against the door. He was bugging and who could blame him?

"You okay?" Jude asked.

"She didn't bite me. But Gram just bought me these shorts." Jabari showed Jude the rip.

"I'm sorry. Usually she's scared of her own shadow." Seeing Pookie like that freaked Jude. Okay. It also made him kind of proud.

"That is one whack dog," Jabari said, still trying to catch his breath. "But it must really like you."

Pookie's ears were still flat on her head. *That's right. Just try and hurt him again!*

Jude looped one end of the rope through her collar, then knotted the other to the fence. When he bent to pet her, she did something she'd never done before. She pressed her head against his hand. *Nuzzled*, that was the word. Here came a memory, tiptoeing back. The first time he ever held Spider. When Mom set him in Jude's lap, he was so little Jude was scared to move, but Spider turned his warm fuzzy head so it fit into his cupped hand. Fit just right, like it was meant to be.

Like, *You and me, from now on.*

"What's this?"

Jabari was picking up a balled-up flyer that must've fallen out of Jude's pocket. Jude grabbed it. Jabari grabbed it back. His eyes darted from the paper to Pookie. He gave a low whistle.

"For real? Five hundred—"

"Mute it!" Jude said, like there was anyone around to hear. He pointed to the fortress. When they were inside, he whispered, "I don't know if it's legit."

"News flash. That is definitely the same dog."

"I know but trust me. The owner doesn't look like she's got any kind of money."

"It's worth finding out though, right?"

Jude lay back on the mattress and didn't answer.

"What's its name again?"

"It's her, not it. And her name's Pookie. Or True."

"Pookytroo? Like Pikachu?"

"Never mind."

"Okay," Jabari said. "I get that you like the dog, even though it just tried to eat me. And it likes you back. But it's not yours, dude."

Jude didn't answer.

"Face it. This is uncool. Sooner or later somebody's bound to find out. Man, JD! If your mother does, say your prayers."

Jude crooked his arm over his eyes.

"But now you got an opportunity. You can do the right thing, plus get paid for it. It's tricky, though. I see that. The owner knows you. She knows Spy and your girlfriend, too."

"She's not my—"

"The lady already thinks you're troublemaking punks, so if you show up wanting the reward money, she's going to wonder what the deal is and it won't go well." Jabari stroked his chin like some wise old man on a mountaintop. "No way you two can return that dog."

Jude began to feel like he was in a space capsule, experiencing zero gravity. His arms, his legs, his head—everything grew lighter.

"True," he said. Lighter and lighter, till he weighed nothing at all. "I guess that settles it. No way I can bring her back."

"To claim the bucks, you need help." Jabari thumped his chest. "Talk about good timing."

Jude slammed back to earth.

And then his phone rang.

"That her?" Jabari tried to see. "Your dudette?"

Jude scrambled past him out into the yard.

"Hey," he said into the phone. "What's up?"

"You aren't answering my texts. I just wanted to make sure everything's okay."

"Why are you whispering?"

"Nap time."

There was sudden heavy breathing, and then he heard Sophie asking who Gladys was talking to. Was it Spy? Was he coming over? Did he want to play with her?

"Shh! Quiet!" Gladys said. "Not you, Jude."

"It is her, isn't it?" Jabari was up in his face, making kissy noises. Jude shoved him, and Pookie barked.

"Who's that?" Gladys said. "What's going on?"

"Quiet, girl," he said. "Not you, Gladys."

"Is everything all right?"

"Why are you even asking me that?" he said. "Don't you trust me?"

"Huh? Of course. I mean, of course."

"Good. I'm kind of busy so—"

"Wait! I need to ask you something."

"Not now, okay?"

"All right." She hesitated. "It's better if we talk about it in person anyway."

Jabari pretended to faint.

"Make sure True has enough water," she went on. Boss of the universe! "I'll do my best to get there tomorrow but— Sophie! Sophie Myers, give me back my phone this instant!"

"Hello?" Sophie said. "Hello?"

"Do what Gladys tells you!" he ordered Sophie, then clicked off.

"Dude!" Jabari said. "You kiss her yet?"

"Lay off, you walking pile of dog food!"

Jabari went dead serious. "When we get the reward, we'll split it with her. That's only fair."

Gladys

S ugar, your patience is rewarded at last," Mama announced at dinner. "Angela decided she hates being a shampoo girl. She wants to come back to work here, and I told her she can start tomorrow."

Even though ditz-brain Angela didn't deserve her job back, and even though before long she'd decide she wanted to become a fashion model or something else improbable and quit again, this was still the best news Gladys had heard in forever.

"You can enjoy the last few days of summer vacation after all," Mama said.

"Let's kick it off with a family movie night," Dada said.

Mama made her famous cheese popcorn, and they let Gladys choose the movie. It was one she'd been wanting to see, but her mind kept wandering. Why had Jude sounded so strange on the phone? Why had he asked if she trusted him? If he didn't know the answer to that by now, he never would.

The film was good but she lost track of what was happening. Dada fell asleep, mouth open, head lolling. Gladys turned to roll her eyes at Mama and realized she was asleep, too. They'd barely made it twenty minutes in before they were both dead to the world.

Her phone vibrated.

Left her water & food should be alright
U sounded weird before

She waited. After a while, the little circles bubbled up again.

My mom wont come out of her room

The back of her throat grew tight. She looked at her father, worn out from his job at Crooked River. A spot on the back of his hand was still puckered and red from where he'd gotten burned dipping candles. She looked at her mother, who in spite of everything was giving Angela yet another chance. Her parents didn't give up. Not on themselves, not on other people. Even when life wasn't fair, they kept believing and hoping and trying again. It was like a habit they couldn't break, no matter what.

Over the years, Mama had coaxed lots of sprouts out of bad habits. Pacifiers, booger-eating, biting other kids. Once she'd had a little girl who pulled out her own hair. That was hard to see and even harder to understand, but Mama slowly, patiently helped her stop. Adults, though. It was much harder to get them to break habits, Mama said. Adults could hang on to their habits like life preservers in a raging sea.

Trusting Gladys was one of her parents' habits. Even though they shouldn't. Even though she didn't deserve it anymore.

Gladys carefully slipped out from between them and went to the kitchen.

So sorry, she texted. *I know u feel bad*
U understand?
For sure. Talk about it tomorrow?

He didn't answer that.

Jude

That girl liked understanding things.

But she was never going to understand him. The proof was: she trusted him.

Guess whose fault that was? Hers, right? Because trust was all about having things in common. When it came to him and her, the list of things they shared was exactly one word long.

And they couldn't even agree on whether the word was *Pookie* or *True*.

The light from Mr. Peters's kitchen window painted a long stripe across the backyard grass. Jude lay down in it. He had a choice to make. He needed it to be the right one.

But what if there was no right choice? What if no matter what he did, it was wrong?

Something moved in Mr. Peters's yard. Turning his head, Jude spied a skunk. It waddled along, then all of a sudden stuck its nose to the ground and started digging. It spun around and dug another hole, tearing up Mr. Peters's grass like its life depended on it. Maybe it did. Plus—whoa. Babies. Three skunk babies, following their mother, hoping for a tasty skunk treat.

Jude jumped up. He felt bad watching them wreck Mr. Peters's nice grass. He should scare them off.

But. Skunks.

He looked up at the sky. Tonight, instead of the stars he could only see the empty spaces in between.

Then he got another text.

This one from Jabari.

Gladys

When Gladys came downstairs in the morning, Angela was sitting on the couch reading some sprouts a story. She waved at Gladys as if nothing had happened. As if she'd never left them in the lurch for her own selfish reasons. The definition of a hypocrite! Gladys managed a one-finger wave back.

She paused in the kitchen doorway. Dada and Mama stood close, softly talking. Gladys watched Mama touch his bearded cheek, then rest her head on his shoulder. They both looked sad. Before Gladys could speak, Mama sensed her there, the way she always did. She tossed her braid back and switched on a too-bright smile.

"Someone got a good sleep! How about a smoothie?"

"Got big plans now that Angela's back?" Dada chimed in.

What was wrong? She wanted to ask, but what if it was about her? Mateo gave a wail.

"Suza!" Angela called. "We got a diaper emergency here and this guy won't let me change him!"

Mama hurried into the living room, but Dada followed Gladys outside. He gave her a granola bar, then, holding his ridiculous hat in one hand and to-go mug in the other, he watched her climb onto her bike.

"How do you like that," he said.

"Huh?"

"Look where your knees hit. You've gotten too big for that bike!"

Too big was a phrase that never appeared in the same sentence as *Gladys*.

"You need a twenty incher, maybe even a twenty-four. Somebody's had a growth spurt." He put his hat on, then swept it off in a courtly bow. "Nicely done, my good lady."

"Stop it, Dada," she said, but in spite of herself, she was relieved he was making his corny jokes again.

"We'll hit the police sale next month and buy the newest bike they got." He set her helmet on her head. "I always said, small on the outside, mighty on the inside. But you're getting mighty inside and out."

Dada didn't ask where she was going. He probably figured Mama already knew, or else he simply trusted her. He was wrong either way but, as Gladys rode off, she realized he was right about the bike. It really was too small. It crimped and cramped. She stood up on the pedals, wondering if this was a sign.

A *portent*. An *omen*. The universe—not the uni*worse*—trying to tell her something.

For the first time in days, the cloud of worry lifted enough for her to think clearly. Even if they took True to the shelter—and this was an *if* so big, Gladys could hardly see around it—even if they did, in order to surrender her they'd have to claim they were her owners. They might not get away with lying and anyway, it wouldn't be fair to True. Lying betrayed her very name.

Yet they couldn't truthfully say she was their dog until they had proof she'd been abandoned. Jude didn't care about proof anymore. He just wanted to keep True, no matter what. He hadn't seen the woman that day, standing petrified beneath the pine tree.

Petrified. The word could mean something living, like a tree, that had been turned to stone. Or it could mean . . .

Gladys stopped her bike and took out her phone. Pulling up her dictionary app, she read that petrified could also mean *horrified, scared, terrified.*

Gladys put her phone back and pedaled on. Now she began to understand something else. All this time, she'd been worried not just about True, but also, deep down, about the woman. In the nightmare, as the tree bark closed over her, she'd tried hard to speak. *Save me!* she'd struggled to say. *Save me please!*

The last time Gladys had seen her, the woman had stood so still, gazing down at the empty dog dishes as if she was the one who was lost. What if she'd realized too late that she should have treated True better? She'd been cruel and unloving but maybe, once True was gone, she regretted it.

There was good in everybody, Mama said. Never give up searching for it.

What if True had been the last bit of good in the woman's life? What if True wasn't the only one who needed saving?

Gladys stopped her bike.

She could say she'd come for her green hat. In an innocent voice, she could inquire where the dog was.

The woman had sworn that if she saw Gladys again, she'd eat her raw.

But what if Mama was right?

For herself, for True, for everyone, Gladys needed to find out. She turned her bike around.

Jude

True danced on her hind legs, tangling herself in her rope, trying to lick Jude's face. As they started down the driveway, she kept turning to look at him. Cheesing like, *You and me, right?*

She trotted along the sidewalk, no idea what he and Jabari had planned. She was so happy. An engine of joy.

He knew she wasn't trying to make him feel rotten.

He was doing that all by himself.

☀

Gladys

Mrs. Marsh's house already had a colorful fall wreath on the door. She was the kind of teacher who really got into seasonal decor. Gladys zipped past the house, then hopped off her bike and leaned it against the chain-link fence.

The lawn chairs were gone from the driveway. The curtains were gone from the windows. Not only that. The tree lawn was heaped with trash bags. On top of the pile sat a motorcycle helmet. In the grass lay a murdered cigarette butt.

She was moving out.

Or she already had.

In her confusion, Gladys thought she heard True barking in the distance. Which was impossible. Nerves—it was her nerves. It was all the emotions tumbling through her one after the other: surprise, confusion, worry. And now, knowing True really belonged to her and Jude: relief, elation, the satisfaction of being proved right.

But out of nowhere another feeling rolled in. A feeling so big and powerful, it squashed all the others.

Fury! How could that woman do it? How could she, too, leave True behind?

Gladys's green hat lay in the dirt beside the doghouse. She couldn't stand to see it there, and she hooked her toe in a chain link and started to climb the fence. But now she heard another painful bark, this time definitely not her imagination. Gripping the fence she turned, and her brain could not process what her eyes saw.

Down the street and headed this way, a kid who looked like he was made of pipe cleaners led True on a rope. True was straining backward, practically dislocating his arm. They were still half a block away, but it was clear True recognized where they were headed. Gladys watched in disbelief as True went up on her hind legs, skittering around. The boy tried to tug her forward, but she flattened herself on the sidewalk, popped back up, wrapped herself and him in her rope. True's eyes rolled. She growled, fangs flashing.

"Help!" the kid yelled over his shoulder. "Jude!"

Gladys lost her grip and tumbled. Falling falling falling . . . nothing and no one to catch her till . . . *thud.*

Sprawled on the ground under the monstrous pine tree, Gladys heard more footsteps come running. And then, thank goodness, she heard Jude to the rescue.

"It's okay, girl," he said. "It's okay!"

"Gaa! Don't let it bite me! Gaa!"

"You're scaring her! Quit yelling! It's okay, girl! It's okay. You all right?"

"You asking me or the dog? What the—? It peed my new kicks! Gross! Disgusting!"

"Jabari. Listen—"

"If this is a five-hundred-dollar dog I'm LeBron James."

"I changed my mind. Give me the rope."

Gladys sat up. Through the fence she could see the boys from the knees down. Poor True cowered behind Jude, tail clamped between her legs.

"I can't take her back there. Look how freaked she is."
Jude's voice was low and calm, his talking-to-True voice.

"Dude!" Jabari's voice was a turkey squawk. "We agreed!"

"I know. But I can't."

"Yeah you can!"

"I won't."

"Don't punk me! After all this? After I almost got bit two
times and my school shoes got peed?"

Gladys darted a look back at the house. If the woman was
still there, she'd have come out by now.

"Five hundred bucks!" Jabari said. "Five. Hundred. Bucks."

"You need hearing aids? I changed my mind. Give me the
rope."

"You're breaking your word again, just like with the fortress! Why'd I even trust you?" Jabari stamped his foot. "Your
word—you know what? It's not worth spit!"

That got Gladys on her feet. "Don't talk to him like that!"

Both boys whirled around, faces slack with astonishment.
Jabari stumbled back and almost fell over True, who gave a
piercing yelp. His head swiveled from the dog to Gladys.

"Who are you?"

"No, who are *you*?" Gladys started to climb the fence, but
her shoe got stuck in one of the links. "What do you think
you're doing to our dog?"

"Gladys!" Jude cried. "What . . . how . . ."

"Give me a hand," she said.

"This is messed up," Jabari said. "This is beyond messed
up."

"Hold the freaking rope!" Jude ordered, starting toward
Gladys.

But no sooner did Jude hand over the rope than True

bolted, yanking free from Jabari and charging into the street, colliding with Mrs. Marsh, who toppled against a parked car with a shrill cry.

"No!" she commanded, in the ringing voice reserved for her worst-behaved students. "Bad dog! Bad dog!"

Mrs. Marsh only scared True more. The dog flew down the street, trailing the rope. As Jude helped Gladys over the fence, she felt the chain link dig into her lower leg. Her shoe caught on the top rail and fell off, but the second he set her down, they both raced after True.

"True!"

"Pookie!"

The dog rounded the corner onto Front Street.

"Munchkins!"

"True!"

"Pookie!"

A car honked, brakes squealed.

But by the time Jude, the world's worst runner, and Gladys, limping, finally reached the corner, True had vanished.

Jude

This time, he was ready to search all day, all night, forever. Because he had to find her. *Had to.*

And because the longer they searched, the longer he could put off explaining to Gladys.

Gladys

Gladys and Jude sat on the picnic table behind the old church. They had searched forever, without finding a trace.

Her leg had a jagged cut. He'd gone to the corner store for a bottle of water to clean it.

"That fence was rusty," he said. "You could get tetanus."

Fallen leaves littered the table and the grass. They were all different shapes. The tree had an identity problem. Gladys, holding the unopened bottle of water, rubbed her eyes.

What had just happened?

"So," she said. "So that was Jabari?"

"Uh-huh."

"The one you built the fortress with?"

"Uh-huh."

"He found True there?"

"I guess."

Gladys touched a finger to her cut. Jude wasn't telling her everything. He wasn't even looking at her. His head was bowed and his arms hung down between his knees. He looked like someone waiting to get punished.

This was much worse than seeing him angry.

"But . . ." She set down the water bottle and picked up a fallen leaf. It was shaped like a ghost, holding up its ghostly arms. "I don't understand."

"He . . . he wanted to return Pook."

It was her turn to grow quiet. She tried to think, but her brain began to go places she didn't want it to.

"I still don't get it, Jude. Why'd you let him? Is that what you meant when you said you changed your mind?" When he didn't answer, she tried to help him. "Or . . . was he just trying to prank you? That would be a really evil prank. Is Jabari evil? Is that why you're not friends anymore?"

Jude shoved himself up from the picnic table. She was sure he'd kick something, or throw something, or curse Jabari out. She almost hoped he would. Instead he carefully set her bike, which they'd gone back to get, along with her shoe, upright. He looked ridiculously big standing next to it, but also . . . Was *weak* the word? It couldn't be, not for Jude. Her mouth started talking again, trying to put words to this, trying to make sense out of it.

"And what did he mean about five hundred dollars? Is he delusional? Plus. Plus, what he said about your word not being worth spit? That was disgusting. Also completely untrue. He deserved to have his shoes peed on. I wish True had pooped on them. He—"

"Could you stop?"

The expression on his face turned her tongue to stone.

"Jabari was right. I was breaking my word. To him. To you." He inhaled. "Most of all, to Pookie."

He reached into his back pocket, the pocket where he used to carry the tree book, and pulled out a crumpled piece of paper. He smoothed it out on the picnic table, then stepped back as if she was a bomb about to explode.

Gladys read the words. She looked at the photo. The leaf fell from her hand, spun a slow spiral to the ground. Her tongue lay petrified in her mouth.

"I know," he said. "You don't have to say it because I already know. Okay? Okay?"

Gladys didn't realize she'd jumped off the table till she was eye level with his chest. She pulled back her arm and socked him with all her might, directly in his middle. Which was hard as a rock. As a tree trunk.

"Gladys," he said, and his voice was so sad.

She couldn't bear to look at him. She couldn't bear to be near him. She couldn't even bear to watch him breathe. She stalked away, then spun around and climbed onto the picnic bench so she towered over him.

"You were going to betray her."

He nodded, miserable.

"Behind my back. Without telling me."

"It's a lot of money."

Mama had a grater she used for shredding cheese. It always gave Gladys the creeps to watch. One moment the cheese was firm and the next it was reduced to thin, limp strips. That was how Gladys felt now. Shredded.

She should have known he wasn't her real friend. Why didn't she know? What was wrong with her? How could she have believed that he wanted to save True as much as she did? Maybe even more than she did? How could she have believed he cared? Not just about True but about their friendship, too? She was so stupid. She was the stupidest girl ever born. She didn't know anything about anything that mattered at all.

"The woman isn't even there anymore," she said, sinking down onto the table. "She moved away."

"Just like her to offer a reward, then leave town before she had to pay it."

"Maybe that's how True got out. Maybe she was packing and didn't pay attention. Maybe True saw a chance to escape."

To escape but not go far. Because she hoped they'd find her.

He stared up into the confused tree. He still hadn't asked why she'd been at the house. He didn't know what she'd been thinking—that the best thing for True was to bring her to the shelter. This was the secret she'd kept from him.

After all this time, after everything they'd been through, what did they really know about each other?

Gladys wrapped her arms around herself.

"What should we do?" She hated saying *we*. It felt like another lie.

Jude didn't say anything. Of course he didn't say anything! But then he did.

"I wish you'd wash that cut. It looks like it hurts."

Gladys's eyes burned with tears. Her leg did hurt. It hurt, but not nearly as badly as her heart did. It had all turned out so wrong. Neither of them had given True what she needed. No wonder she ran away. No wonder she didn't come back when they called.

Jude

He took the neighborhood and Gladys took the fortress. That was her idea. It was easier for her to get away for longer periods of time, now that his mother was home all day, plus she claimed no-man's-land didn't scare her anymore.

Every day they searched, and every night they sent each other a one-word text.

Nothing

Nothing

The only communication they had.

"Let's go to Soapie's house," Spider begged. "I wanna. I wanna. I—"

"We can't."

"Why? Why not?"

"Because. A monster ate her."

Spider slid his thumb into his mouth.

"Not really!" Jude said. "Monsters aren't real."

But Spider just sucked his thumb, like he knew otherwise.

. . .

Jabari said that while Jude and Gladys went chasing after True, Mrs. Marsh demanded to know what exactly was going on. In full sentences, please. Jabari made up a big story about

Gladys starting a dog-walking business and him and Jude trying to help her. When Mrs. Marsh said that dog looked like the one that used to live here, Jabari said actually it belonged to his grandma who was keeping it for his cousin who had to get rushed to the hospital. Burst appendix. Jabari put so much hot sauce on the story, Mrs. Marsh must have bought it, because she didn't call their parents on them.

Good old Jabari.

. . .

Jude went back to Pookie's house once. It had a FOR RENT sign on the lawn now.

Peering over the fence, Jude identified the big tree as an Eastern white pine. Same species as his. Amazing. He wondered who'd planted it. He wondered if they'd known it would grow so massive, taking over the yard, dwarfing the house, becoming the biggest, most alive thing in sight.

The tree nodded in the breeze. A weird little green hat that had to be Gladys's lay near the empty doghouse. He went through the gate. Why the freak had she climbed the fence instead of using the gate? Just like her to make things more complicated.

He took the hat to her house and left it by the front door.

Gladys

Mama, of course, had demanded to know how Gladys hurt her leg, and when Gladys claimed she'd fallen off her bike, and Dada said no wonder, that bike was too small, Mama wouldn't let her ride it anymore. Gladys could have argued, but she didn't. All the fight had gone out of her.

Instead, every day for the next four days, she walked the endless distance to the fortress, where she filled True's water dish and put whatever meat or cheese she'd smuggled from the house into the food dish. The next day the dishes were empty, not that this meant anything. Hideous rats or gruesome possums could be gobbling the food.

School began in three days. *School!* One of those small words with XL impact. Would Chickie still sit with her at lunch? Would they be partners on projects? Gladys had barely thought of her old friend for days. Had Chickie thought of her?

Mama made a last-minute offer to take Gladys to Goodwill and Aunt Annie's Attic, but it wouldn't be the same without Chickie. Besides, what did it even matter what she wore on the first day? School had never seemed more irrelevant.

That afternoon, when Gladys got home, tired and heartsick from the fortress, Mama and Sophie were sitting on the front steps. Mrs. Myers had connived to have Mama watch

Sophie, even though it was Sunday. When Sophie saw Gladys, she leaped up and glommed on.

"Gladys! Hi! Hi!" She whispered into Gladys's ear, "Did you go see Spy?"

"Not today." Gladys tried but failed to pry her off.

"When can we go see him?"

"We can't."

"How come?"

"Because."

"'Cause is no answer. Ms. Suza says."

Gladys looked to her mother for help, but Mama only nodded, agreeing with Sophie.

"Because . . ." Tears pushed at the backs of her eyes but Gladys blinked them away. "Spy and Jude aren't our friends anymore."

Sophie's head jerked back. "They're not?"

"No."

Sophie let go of Gladys and slid to the ground. Sprouts woke up each morning expecting the day to brim with new delights. Their goofy little hearts were wide open. Gladys hated being the one to tell Sophie the hard, withering truth. Life wasn't all wonderful. Sometimes it was cruel and stingy. Sometimes it gave you a gift, then snatched it back again.

"I'm so sad," Sophie said.

"I'm so sorry," Mama said.

Jude

I stopped after church and got you a bunch of school supplies." Auntie Jewel set a bag down on the coffee table, then frowned, hands on hips. "How long you two been vegging in front of that TV? Never mind. Get some fresh air. I'll be out soon as your mom and I finish arguing." She winked and shooed them outside.

Next door, Mr. Peters was sitting in a lawn chair. The drink holder had a tall glass of something with ice. By his feet, an old-fashioned radio with an antenna played some lame E-Z listening stuff. Even wearing his button-down shirt and hard shoes, he looked almost chill.

"Hello, boys!" he called in that deep voice.

A ladder leaned against Mr. Peters's gutters. Like it had his name on it, Spider spidered up.

"Careful!" Mr. Peters jumped to his feet.

"Get down here, buddy." Jude kept his voice calm. More or less.

Guess who obeyed?

Guess who almost fainted with surprise?

Mr. Peters ran a finger inside his collar. Mom and Auntie Jewel had started arguing, their voices spilling out the open bedroom window.

"I turned off the light that bothered her," Mr. Peters told Jude.

"I know. Thanks."

"The skunks have been having a party on the lawn." He pointed. Holes the size of golf balls. The grass around them all brown. "Digging for grubs."

"I'm sorry," Jude said.

Mr. Peters glanced at the window to Mom's bedroom, where the sisters were getting into it.

"I haven't seen her go to work," he said.

"Good Sam laid her off."

"I was afraid of that."

The voices got louder. It was embarrassing. Jude didn't believe in being embarrassed by his family, but he was.

"My aunt wants her to come work for their realty company," he explained. "But Mom would rather lick an eyeball."

"Your mother's an independent person." Mr. Peters sat back down. Mom was telling Auntie Jewel their mother must've dropped her on her head when she was a baby. "Sometimes anger's more hopeful than sadness," he went on. "Sadness just lies down, but anger puts up its dukes." Inside, a door slammed. Mr. Peters winced. "Not saying it's easy to live next door to her."

"Or with her," said Jude.

Mr. Peters smiled. The smile was small and neat, just like him.

"She cares about you boys," he said. "And why shouldn't she? You're a fine young man, a good role model to your brother. And Spider..." Mr. Peters paused, trying to think of something good to say about Spider, who'd grabbed his radio and was spinning the dial.

"I'm sorry about your lawn, Mr. Peters."

"Well. I'll tell you a secret." He gave a small cough. Smoothed an invisible wrinkle on his shirt. "I was getting sick and tired of taking care of it."

Gladys

Tuesday night, the night before the first day of school, Gladys opened her dictionary, longing for the comfort it always offered.

There, marking her place in the *C* section, was the mitten leaf Jude had given her.

Care.

Gladys turned the pages.

Carnage.

Castigate.

Catastrophe.

The pages rustled, whispered. She turned back to *care*.

Jude cared about True, but he cared about his family, too. He'd made up his mind to help his mother and brother, even though giving up True had to break his heart.

She ran her finger down the long list of definitions for the humble little word. She tried to read them all, but the words grew blurry. She rested her cheek on the page.

It was hard to blame anyone for caring so deeply.

Not hard. *Impossible.*

Jude

He stood on the edge of the blacktop, waiting for the first bell to ring. Now and then he glimpsed Gladys near the school door. But she was so small, the swarms of kids swallowed her up. He shifted his backpack, heavy with the supplies Auntie Jewel had bought. Out on the sidewalk a dog barked. He automatically spun around, even though he already knew it wasn't her. Pookie had taught him every dog had its own voice.

Jabari showed up and they did their handshake.

"There she is." Jabari pointed.

"So?"

"So?"

"She doesn't want to talk to me."

"You sure?"

☼

Gladys

The bell was never going to ring. She was going to stand here forever, desolate and isolated, while every other kid in town shouted and laughed in mindless first-day excitement.

Except him. Across the blacktop, he looked like a prisoner awaiting the firing squad.

"Hi."

Gladys was startled to discover Chickie standing beside her. *Startled* being a totally inadequate adjective.

"Hi," she said back.

"I like your hair that way," Chickie said.

Mama had insisted on fixing it this morning, and it did look nice, Gladys knew.

"Thank you," she said. And then she lied. "I like your shirt."

"You lie." Chickie smiled. She hesitated a moment, then added, "Well, see you in class."

"Okay." Gladys watched her former best friend wander toward a pod of girls dressed in generic Target outfits.

Out on the street a dog woofed. Gladys stood on tiptoe, though she already knew it wasn't True.

Jude

When Jude got home that afternoon, Spider was zonked on the couch. Thumb in his mouth, other hand clutching the T. rex he'd stolen from Gladys's house. Jude could hear Mom in her room, talking on the phone. He was trying to find something to eat when she came into the kitchen. He got ready for her to grill him on the first day of school.

Instead she opened the refrigerator, took out a carton of eggs.

"You're not going to believe this. Miss Edith at Good Sam? My doily diva? I've been calling to check up on her." Mom started cracking eggs into a bowl. "She says things have gone so downhill there, her nephew's moving her out to live with him. She has this big-shot nephew who owns his own contracting business over in Middleton." She whisked the eggs with milk. "I actually met him a few times."

Jude watched her melt butter in a frying pan, pour in the eggs. This was already the most she'd said to him since she got fired. Not to mention, she'd cooked exactly nothing. He had zero idea why she was talking about some rich contractor two towns over, but guess who wasn't about to interrupt her?

"So it turns out she's been telling him how unfair they treated me. I guess he got sick of listening to her because…" She slid the eggs onto a plate and set it on the table along with two forks. "He just called. He says he has a sudden opening in his office and am I interested."

"What? Really?"

"You're catching flies, mister." She got the ketchup, pulled out a chair. "Sit down. Nothing's worse than cold eggs."

"That's amazing, Mom." He fell into the chair. "That's like . . . like the payoff for how hard you worked at Good Sam. How good you were to the residents."

"Don't get too excited." She poked at her scar. "It's an office job. I don't know much about jobs where you get to sit down."

"But you're smart. You learn fast."

"I must've said something right because he wants me to come in Friday to talk." She squirted ketchup. They both loved ketchup. Suddenly her eyes bugged. "I'll have to ask Jewel to watch Spy! I didn't even want her to know about this. If I don't get the job, she'll love feeling sorry for me. Nothing makes her happier."

"Mom, Auntie Jewel cares about you and you know it."

"Listen to you!"

Spider wandered in, rubbing his eyes. Mom fed him a bite, then all of a sudden remembered. She jabbed her fork in Jude's direction.

"How was your first day? Say excellent, mister, or you are in big trouble!"

Gladys

Mama and Dada wanted to hear every detail of her first day, and it was exhausting, like trying to translate an incredibly complex experience for people who spoke another language. By the time dinner was over, Gladys couldn't wait to retreat to her room.

"I have a ton of homework," she said. Her parents looked confused.

"On the first day?"

"I'm afraid it's going to be a rough year."

She closed her bedroom door and threw herself onto the bed. She punched up her pillow and lay on her back, her favored position for thinking and pondering, but tonight her mind was empty. The school day had stretched long and lonesome as the tundra, and by the time she'd walked to the fortress and put food she'd saved from lunch in the empty pan, then walked home, looking and listening for True every step of the way, she had nothing left.

"Glad?" Dada knocked, then peeked around the edge of the door. "Can I come in?"

Without waiting for an answer, he sat on the edge of the bed. He picked up a stuffed cow he'd once brought her from the Crooked River gift shop.

"Must have been a moooooonster of a first day," the cow said.

As if he'd flung open a door marked SADNESS, tears began to roll down her cheeks and into her ears, where they tickled in a disgusting way. Dada sat on the edge of the bed, his hands on his knees.

"I'm listening," he said.

"It's not just today," she whispered, trying not to cry. Really cry. "It's more."

"You want to tell me?"

She loved him so much. Him and Mama—she loved them with every bit of her being.

"No," she said. "I mean yes. But . . ." She rolled over and buried her face in her damp, disgusting pillow. "It's a lot more."

"Mooooving in," the cow said, as Dada swung his legs onto the bed and leaned back. The cow nuzzled her ear. "Whatever it is, we can fix it."

"I don't think so." The lump in her throat was so big, she had to push the words around it. "Because . . . you might not want . . . And what if? You think you know but you don't. And when you do, you won't . . ."

"Take a breath, Glad."

"I'm not a baby anymore. Like I was when you adopted me."

"I did notice that."

"I'm different. A lot of stuff about me is wrong."

"Hey!"

"It is! You don't know."

"I think I—"

"What if you made a mistake? What if you picked the wrong kid?"

Dada gripped her shoulders and sat her up so abruptly, her teeth clicked together and her breath caught in her throat. Her gentle father wore a fierce expression she'd never seen before. She still clutched the pillow, but he tossed it aside to pull her close. He was quiet a long moment, and then words came tumbling out.

"For years, Mama and I wanted a child. Like a person wants to eat or breathe, we wanted one. But we had to wait. A long time, and that was hard. The hardest. Sometimes while we were waiting, it felt like it might never happen."

Gladys knew this. They'd told her this. But what he said next—she didn't know that.

"It felt like, as much as we wanted it, maybe we weren't meant to be parents." His breath was hot against her wet ear. "Maybe something was wrong with us, and the universe was telling us no."

"Dada!" She drew back to look at him in disbelief.

"That's how it felt. And I'll tell you right now. Nothing in my life or Mama's ever felt worse than that."

"But—"

"But then came the day we met you. And we both knew all the waiting was for a reason. We had to wait so long because no one else would do."

Gladys's head thunked against his chest.

"Dada, I know you say that, but—"

"I don't *say* it. I can't even say it. The way we love you goes deeper than any words I got."

She looked up into his face. The fierceness was still there, but softer, a tender fierceness.

"I'll tell you something else," he said. "Loving another person isn't always easy. There'll be a time you wish for different parents—yeah, yeah, you will! But Mama and me, we're never going to wish for another kid."

Gladys leaned against him. Would he say all this if he knew what she'd been doing? If he had any idea of all the secrets she was keeping? Something—maybe it was false hope but still—something told her the answer was yes.

They were quiet till Dada picked up the cow again.

"Moooooving on." He grimaced at his own bad joke. "Guess I might as well tell you now. I was putting it off because I didn't want to spoil your first day of school. But today was my last day at Crooked River. They let a bunch of us go."

"That's unjust! You grew a terrible beard! You wore that terrible hat! You sold overpriced souvenirs!"

"Yeah." Dada nodded. "It wasn't exactly my dream job."

He tried to smile—he did smile, but only with his mouth. Now he'd have to hunt for work again, some other job he'd dislike but would be grateful to find, and in the meantime, money would get even tighter. Gladys took his big hand between both of hers. If only she could make him her old, happy Dada again. If only she knew how to make everything as simple as it used to be!

He tucked her hair behind her ear. "I have something for you," he said. "I used my gift shop discount one last time."

He pulled out a square wrapped in tissue. Here she was wishing she could give him happiness but instead, he was giving her something. When she folded back the paper, she found two ornate silver buckles.

"You can attach them to a hat or shoes or whatever," he said, showing her how.

"They're beautiful!" She threw her arms around him. "Thank you, Dada."

"You're welcome," he said.

Her phone, lying on her night table, began to ring. He picked it up, glanced at the name, then passed it to her. Standing up, he said, "Tell him I said hi," and slipped out of the room.

Jude

Three rings.
Four.

Jude stood in his front yard. It turned out Auntie Jewel and Uncle Hal were leaving for a "getaway" tomorrow so Auntie Jewel couldn't watch Spider on Friday. Mom was already nervous about the interview and now she was pacing the house saying stuff like *The one time I ask her for something!* and *Wouldn't you know it?* and *Now what?*

Five rings.

"Hello, Jude," Gladys said.

Quick, making sure he didn't give her false hope, he answered, "I still didn't find her. I'm not quitting though."

"I know."

"You do?"

"Uh-huh." Gladys's voice was shaky. "And I think I understand why you did what you did. Why you *almost* did it."

Jude stood in the dark, listening as she told him about her father losing another job, and how unfair that was, and how if she had any chance in the universe to make Dada happy, she'd take it.

She didn't hate him. She didn't hate his guts and wish he'd never been born. At least not 100 percent.

A green shoot of hope sprouted inside him.

"About that? Making your parent happy?" He pulled a breath. "I need to ask you a big favor."

. . .

Back inside, Mom sat at the kitchen table. Chin on her hand, staring at her laptop. Even though the screen was blank.

"How am I supposed to find a sitter on such short notice?" she said. "I need to postpone the interview. After I swore I'd be there. Great impression that'll make."

"You can go, Mom. I know somebody who'd love to babysit Spy."

Surprising her—surprising her in a good way—was anything better? After he told her about Ms. Suza, she looked at him. Looked at him like, *Do I know you?* Then she fired up her laptop.

"I gotta practice my keyboarding." She raised a finger. "And you..."

"...gotta do my homework."

"That's right. But first, get over here, mister."

Guess who got a bone-crusher hug?

Gladys

On Friday, she and Jude didn't exactly walk home from school *together*. Jude stayed on the other side of the street, half a block ahead. Which was certainly annoying, but since Gladys had never walked home with a boy before, and since that boy turned out to be Jude, she chose to be magnanimous about it.

At her house, Sophie and Spider were busy with cardboard blocks.

"We're building a fort," Sophie said.

"Fortress," Spider corrected.

Jude and Spider's mother, Diamond, had a job interview. When Jude had asked Gladys if her mother could babysit, a fountain of happiness had gushed up inside her. Now Mama set out a snack as she described the moment Diamond came to drop Spider off.

"Neither of us could believe it," she said, "We already know each other! Diamond helped take care of my mother when she was at Good Sam. Ma didn't like most of the aides— actually, she didn't like a single one of them, except for your mother. She'd make sure Ma got extra pats of butter from the kitchen, and my mother just adored butter!"

Mama smiled, then gave Jude a closer look.

"She was surprised Silas had already been here. I guess you never told her?"

Gladys stared down at the silver buckles gleaming on her shoes. She watched the scuffed-up toe of Jude's basketball shoe dig into the rug.

"I guess I forgot," he said.

"Well. I hope her interview goes well. I told her if she gets the job, I'm more than happy to keep Silas."

"You told her that?" Jude looked up.

"Sophie and I would love nothing better, huh, Soph?"

But she and Spider were too busy destroying the fortress to reply.

Jude

He tried watching Spider sleep. Tried picturing the stars overhead. Said the names of all the trees he could think of, tossed and turned some more, finally gave up. Carrying his shoes, he tiptoed past his mother's shut bedroom door and outside.

Tonight, no stars.

What was he doing, sneaking out again? Just when things were getting better. Mom had said her interview went okay, and Gladys wasn't mad at him anymore.

All the wrong choices he'd made were forgiven. Or at least forgotten. Why risk messing everything up again?

This time make the right choice, he told himself.

You'd think that would be easy.

Jude put on his shoes.

He went up and down on his toes, telling himself to turn around and go back to bed.

Make the choice a smart kid would.

He touched the trunk of his pine tree. Trees had roots holding them down, doing all that work underground. And then they had branches, doing their own thing up in the air and light. Trees needed both parts to live.

He needed his family, anchoring him. But he needed something else, too. Something that was all his.

He stepped out into the dark.

The air was cooler than he'd expected and before he'd gone a block he wished he'd worn his hoodie. He hustled.

"Pook?" he called. "Girl?"

A train was coming. A train was always coming. He could see its circle of light bearing down as he ducked under the barriers, raced across. For a second the light cut him in two. Then dark swallowed him back down.

No-man's-land. Like an idiot he'd forgotten his phone.

"Pookie?" And then, "True?"

The roof of the house was an arrow pointing at the sky.

Up the driveway, around the back.

Her pans lay upside down in the grass. They looked silly, the way kids' toys looked when no kids were around. Gladys had the house's door propped open and he went in, feeling his way in the funky dark. There was his tree book lying on the bed Gladys made. He took it outside, where he peeled back the tarp and lay down on the Beautyrest. Thumbed a few pages, then held the book to his chest and watched clouds streak across the sky. Clouds at night were mysterious. Like, the secret life of clouds.

That giant's hands held back the rest of the world. Whispered, *Hush. Peace. Hush.*

Just a few minutes, then he'd go.

Jude searched the sky, but no star. He wished anyway.

Holding the tree book close, the way he used to hold Army Man, he rolled on his side, pulling himself into a ball. He waited.

He waited.

A sound jerked him awake. How long had he been asleep?

Jude rolled over and the crinkle of the mattress sounded loud as a shout. Overhead, silver clouds raced by. Like his skin had extra sensors, he felt the air parting. Whoever was out there stopped a few feet away, just out of sight.

Jude held his breath.

Waited.

The clouds split. A single star.

Make a wish, Jude.

He shut his eyes. The way his heart chugged, he swore it was getting bigger.

And then he whispered, "Girl?"

A quiet whimper, rising like a question.

He tried to move slow so she wouldn't freak, but moving slow was impossible and besides, as soon as she saw his face Pookie went electric with joy. She head-butted him and he threw his arms around her neck. She licked his face, his hands, his knees. She did her crazy two-legged dance, then threw herself back against him, making a sound he'd never heard before. It reminded him of Spider when he first woke up. That sweet, contented *umm*. Like, *Don't make me leave this dream. Let me stay right here forever.*

He stroked her head and happiness—huge happiness, giant happiness, happiness like who knew it was possible—busted out of him like he was giving off light. Like he was some kind of two-legged star.

Who knew how long they sat like that.

Who knew anything except the two of them, here together in the fortress.

He needed to tell Gladys. She'd flip. She'd lose her mind.

But he didn't have his phone.

Besides, it was the middle of the night.

So he couldn't tell her, not yet. No way. And he should've felt bad, but he didn't. He and Pookie sat there together in the

hush and quiet, watching the sky turn from black to gray, hearing birds start to sing. He could see the leaves on the trees now,
each one edged with light.

He wasn't ready to share Pookie yet. He wanted her all to
himself, like she was his dog. *His*.

At least for a while.

Gladys

*T*unk!
Something hit her window. A befuddled bug, probably. It was very early, the window a pearly gray square. The night had been cool and she pulled the covers up over her head.

She didn't want to wake up. She'd been dreaming she was lost in thick, gloomy woods, stumbling over roots and rocks for what seemed forever, until she spied a light among the trees. She tried to find her way to it, but it kept disappearing in the thickets, only to peek out again, shining even brighter. At last, bone-tired, she came to the mouth of a cave. Chilled as she was, warm as the golden light pouring out appeared, could she trust it? The cave was so deep, she couldn't tell where it ended, or if it ended at all. What if this was the home of a child-eating monster? What if the cave was so deep, she'd get lost and never find her way out?

In the way of dreams, and sometimes real life, the next thing she knew she was inside. The golden light grew arms, strong but gentle arms that wrapped her snug and safe. A voice whispered things she couldn't understand, but as the light warmed her, the whisper spun itself into a single word.

Found.

She squeezed her eyes shut, hating to let the dream go.

Tunk. There it was again. That bug was going to knock itself out.

She lifted her head. A ray of real-life golden light finagled its way between her curtains.

Tunk.

Then.

A bark like nails rattling in a metal bucket.

She threw off the covers and flew to the window.

Jude

He'd never made another human this happy.

Well, maybe Spider. For two minutes.

Not that Spider was fully human.

They were in Gladys's backyard, keeping as quiet as they could so they wouldn't wake her parents. Gladys brought out some water. A bunch of cheese sticks, too. Pookie gobbled them so fast Jude was scared she'd choke. All the while Gladys was telling her how amazing she was, how astonishing and brilliant and extraordinary. The words kept falling, like stars. He imagined them making sparkly piles all around them.

Through the branches of the sycamore, streaks of yellow light.

He borrowed her phone to text his mother that he'd gotten up early to go see Gladys. It was a lame excuse but he prayed she'd swallow it, considering how Ms. Suza was on her good side.

Pookie rested her snout on his knee. He'd thought the massive happiness he'd felt before was a one-time-only deal, but it kept coming back.

They'd found each other. Him and Pookie.

Gladys smiled at the two of them. She was wearing a T-shirt that came down to her knees and her hair stuck out like a mad scientist's. Jude looked at her little hands and more stars fell. He wanted to hold one. Her hand, not a star.

Gladys

True had found her way home.

Before Gladys could think, she reached over and grabbed Jude's hand. He jumped as if she'd given him an electric shock.

Jude

"Gladys? Jude?" It was Ms. Suza. "What in the name of heaven?"

Busted.

Pookie bounced up. Her eyes rolled and her crazy-colored fur bristled along her spine. Ears flat and tail down, she hid under the slide.

He knew how she felt.

"What is going on?" Ms. Suza was pulling a shawl around herself. "Are you all right?"

"Mama! I'm sorry, I was going to tell you eventually. Her name is True. Isn't she beautiful?"

"What are you talking about? Where did that dog come from?"

"She was lost, but she came back! She found her way back to Jude!"

"A stray dog?"

"She doesn't bite," Jude said. "She's just scared now, that's all."

Ms. Suza looked at Pookie, trembling beneath the slide. "I want you both to stand over here next to the door. No arguing! Stay right here till I come back."

Gladys's father stumbled outside then, blinking and scratching his beard. He held the door when Ms. Suza came back with a tray of plates, cups, juice, and hot buttered toast. That toast smelled really, really good. Pookie thought so, too. She edged out from under the slide.

"Sit," Jude said.

And she did.

"Well," Gladys's father said. "Will you look at that."

Ms. Suza poured the juice and set out the toast. Ms. Suza—she was all about taking care of you.

Jude dug in but Gladys was too busy talking. And talking. Jude thought he'd heard her talk a lot before but she was shooting for her personal record. She told her parents everything. Bringing Sophie and Mateo to his house. The lady saying she'd eat them raw. The fortress on the other side of the tracks. When she got to the part about Jude and the reward, she sped up, like she was trying to protect his feelings.

Still, it all added up to one thing: a massive pile of lies she'd told her parents. Who sat there listening. Not interrupting once. He'd never seen anything like it.

An alien. He was an alien on planet Gladys.

Meanwhile, Pookie slunk within striking distance of the toast. Gladys's allergic father sneezed a few times, but he and Ms. Suza didn't say anything as Jude fed Pookie toast bits, then let her lick his fingers. The falling-star happiness showered over him again and for a few moments he forgot everything else.

Then Gladys said something that made him doubt his own ears.

She'd researched animal shelters. She'd been ready to convince Jude they should take True to a no-kill one in the next town.

"What?" He stared at her. "You what?"

"I *was* thinking it," she said. "Past tense, Jude. Because now

I know I was so wrong. I've been wrong about a lot of things, but this was the biggest. You think you found her by chance? No way! You were meant to be together. She knew it way before you did. I told you she was an exceptional dog! True belongs with you, no place else."

He stared at her, her elf face and hyper hair. He knew his own stupid face was turning red and there was nothing he could do to stop it.

"You're good at taking care of things, way better than I am," she told him. "All I ever wanted was…" She looked away, and he watched her choose her words. Find the exact ones to explain what she meant. Explain it to herself, not just him. When she started talking again, her voice was so soft he could hardly hear it.

"I wanted her to love me," Gladys said. "Love me best. I did. But mostly…mostly what I wanted was for her to find the person she was waiting for. The person who'd give her a true, forever home."

Gladys's father reached for her. Her parents were both big, and she looked smaller than ever, settling against him, sheltering in the cave of his arms.

Pookie licked the last of the butter off Jude's fingers. Set her muzzle on his knee. He got super busy scratching that spot between her ears. He didn't want to look at Gladys or her parents. He felt the tears gathering at the backs of his eyes. He knew what was coming next.

But Ms. Suza was watching him. You could try, but you couldn't hold out long against her. He had to look up. There was her face, calm as the moon. But the moon, Jude realized now, always looked a little sad.

"Jude," Ms. Suza said gently. "Here's what I think we need to do. First, find her owner and see if she wants her dog back."

"But Mama!" Gladys busted out. "She skipped town! She abandoned True!"

"Don't forget, she offered a reward."

"I don't care. She's wicked."

"I don't like that word, Gladys. From the way you describe her, she sounds like someone who was badly hurt."

"She hurt True!"

"Someone had hurt *her*. We teach each other how to hurt," Mama said, "just as surely as we teach each other how to love."

"Anyway," Jude said. Rubbing his eyes, pushing back the tears. "It doesn't matter anyway."

"What do you mean?" Gladys cried. "Of course it matters! Don't say that!"

"Why don't you believe me?" He tried one more time to make her understand. "No way I can keep her. This was all for nothing."

Gladys was the one who burst into tears.

Gladys

She and Jude sat in the back seat with True Blue between them. Jude's arm circled the dog's neck like one of them was drowning and the other was a lifeguard, but who knew which was which. Meanwhile, True loved every minute of the short ride. She kept pushing past Jude to stick her head out the window. Grinning, she looked back at them. *Is riding in a car the best thing ever invented or what?*

Jude said his mother had been bitten by a dog when she was young and it scarred her for life. Mama said that with help, people could overcome bad experiences. Gladys said True could melt the heart of the worst dog hater.

But Jude knew his own mother. Once she made up her mind about something, guess who could change it? Nobody, that's who.

Gladys could tell he'd abandoned all hope.

Which made her even more determined to prove him wrong.

Mama had called Jude's mother to say she was driving him home. When they pulled up in front of the house, Diamond was cutting the grass with a push mower that looked as if it belonged in a museum of garden implements. She was red-faced and sweaty and clearly in no mood. The neat-as-a-pin neighbor was outside, too, standing in his yard watching her grunt and shove the mower. He was wringing his hands as if he wanted to say something but didn't dare.

When Diamond saw Mama drive up, she dropped the mower and crossed the grass, wiping her brow and smiling.

"Suza! Thanks for bringing Jude—"

She broke off when True's head jutted out the window. Her face froze in disbelief. True, of course, began to bark. Diamond's hands flew up.

"It's okay, Mom," Jude tried. "It's—"

"Ms. Suza!" The house's front door opened and out flew Spider, waving a broken lightsaber. "You came to *my* house. And you brought Pookie!"

His mother grabbed him and pulled him to her. Her horror was giving way to confusion. Horrified confusion.

"Pookie? You know its name?"

"Her name is True," Gladys said. "True Blue."

Diamond began to tremble.

So did True.

It was possible she peed the car seat.

"Diamond," Ms. Suza said. "The kids have a lot of explaining to do. I mean, a lot. But I promise you this isn't a vicious dog. I'd never trust her anywhere near children if she was."

With that, True squeezed out the window and sprinted away.

"True!"

"Pookie!"

No! Not again! But this time, when they called her, she slowed. By the time she got to the next yard, she stopped.

"Good girl," the neighbor said. His voice was deep as the Atlantic Ocean.

"Good girl." Jude jumped out of the car and ran to kneel beside True. "Good, good girl."

The mothers were talking to each other. Actually, Mama was doing all the talking while Diamond listened, slack-jawed.

"I don't believe we've been introduced," the neighbor said as Gladys joined them on his lawn. Jude, who badly needed lessons in etiquette, was too busy calming True to notice.

"I'm Gladys," she said, "and this is True."

"I'm Mr. Peters, and this is also true."

Mr. Peters bent to get a closer look at True and to Gladys's surprise, True didn't flinch or jump away. Instead, she studied him from under her old-man eyebrows.

"What a fine dog," he said, lifting his matching old-man eyebrows. "Is she yours?"

"She's Jude's. We just need to convince his mother of that fact."

Mr. Peters looked worried.

"I keep trying to explain about my mother," Jude told him. "But Gladys is too stubborn to listen."

"He underestimates *my* mother," Gladys told Mr. Peters. "She's an expert on finding the good in every situation and every person."

"It'll never work," Jude said.

"You don't know."

"Yes I do."

"No you don't. Just think of all the things that have worked so far." She held up her fingers to count them off, but Jude's mother interrupted.

"Mister!" She crooked her finger at him. "Get yourself over here. Now."

Jude

Wish.
Could a wish work with no star in sight?

Gladys

Jude was right.

Gladys hated to admit it, but he was.

No way in this galaxy or any other would his mother let him keep True.

It wasn't because she was mean. Well, she was slightly mean, Gladys was coming to agree. But mainly, Diamond was frightened. To her, dogs were wild beasts capable of attack at any moment, without warning. Inside every dog, no matter how sweet it seemed, lurked the ghost of the one who'd bitten her. When she warned Jude and Spider about dogs, she was only trying to protect her children the way any good, if misguided, mother would.

It wasn't as if True liked Diamond much, either. In fact, Gladys was pretty sure that, given half a chance, she would pee on Jude's mother's shoes.

When Diamond beckoned Jude, True tried to follow him, but Gladys made her sit. Her eyes, though. Her sky-blue, star-blue eyes. Nothing could stop them following him everywhere he went. She whimpered pathetically, and from the look on Mr. Peters's face, Gladys guessed that he felt just as helpless.

"Jude's a fine boy," Mr. Peters told True. "You and I agree."

His grass, which had looked so perfect the last time she saw it, was a mess of brown spots and dirt divots.

"I've lost the battle of the lawn," he said, following her gaze. Everything the man said sounded as if it should be engraved in stone. Without seeming to realize it, he'd started scratching True in her precise favorite spot. "But as it turns out, I may have won the war. I was spending every blessed minute taking care of this yard, Gladys. Now that I've surrendered, I've got time for other things."

"It's still a very pretty yard."

"Thank you."

"It's imperfect in a pleasant way."

"I appreciate that."

Mama had finished her copious explaining and cajoling. She'd turned to Silas and his cockeyed lightsaber, leaving True's fate up to Jude and his mother. Diamond's arms were tightly folded and her jaw was set in a way that radiated *NO*. Even from Mr. Peters's lawn, Gladys could see that Jude, who'd barely said a word back, was losing.

Mr. Peters rested his hand lightly atop True's head, and True let him. She'd made up her doggy mind. Here was another human she could trust.

Dogs knew. Just like babies, they knew.

Gladys, Jude, and True had lost the battle. But maybe— maybe not the war.

"Mr. Peters," Gladys said, "could I ask you something?"

Jude

"You get it, don't you?" Mom asked him. "Even if I liked dogs—and I'm sorry, Jude, but that is never going to happen in this lifetime—even if I could stand to have a dog in the house, it's the totally wrong time. I'm really hoping to get that job. I need to put money into the car, I need to pay for day care for Spy. I've got way too much to figure out."

This wasn't her usual *I say so. End of story.* Mom was actually trying to explain.

"You were really trying to get that reward for us?" She brushed the hair back from his brow. "Mister, that was a loco thing to do." Her dented smile. "I still appreciate it."

He worked his mouth but no words came out. If only he knew the right ones! Mom rested her hands on his shoulders.

"You meant to do the right thing. That counts. I shouldn't say this, but it makes me proud. I'm proud of you, and your dad would..." She touched her forehead to his, then stepped back. "I have a chance to make things better for us. And it's going to work out, I promise. Up to the moon and stars, I promise things will get better."

He wanted to tell Mom *Okay. Okay.* But he couldn't. Things couldn't get better without True.

"Ahem," Gladys said.

Jude and his mother both spun around. She and Mr. Peters

stood a few feet behind them, True at their feet. Tail swishing, mouth open like, *Guess what?*

"You." Mom eyed Gladys. "The partner in crime."

Gladys switched on her high-beam smile. Which only made Mom look at her suspiciously. Meanwhile, Mr. Peters pressed his palms together like he might start praying. When Mom turned that suspicious gaze on him, he took a step back. Cleared his throat. Took another step back. He might've turned and run for his life if Gladys hadn't given his shirt sleeve a tug.

"Hello, Diamond," he said.

"Mr. Peters."

"I…uh…" He coughed. "Would you like to borrow my lawn mower? Or I could mow your grass. I wouldn't mind at all."

Mom set her hands on her hips. "Is that what you came over to say?"

Another tug from Gladys.

"We used to have a dog. When my wife was still alive, we had a schnauzer. He was smaller than True but very naughty. She spoiled him, is why." Mr. Peters's big voice thinned. "Peppermint died three months after she did."

Mom's hands slowly slid off her hips.

"She died?" Spider said.

Mr. Peters nodded. Spider handed him his lightsaber.

"Thank you." Mr. Peters clutched the sword. Cleared his throat again. "It's been a long time since I took care of anything."

"Besides your lawn, you mean." Soon as she said it, Mom looked sorry. But Mr. Peters only nodded.

"I think I may be ready to give it another try. Not the lawn, I mean. But caring for *something*." He bent to rub the white stripe between True's eyes.

Mom smiled. Her real smile, like a leaf turning in the breeze.

"Are you saying what I think you're saying, Mr. Peters?"

"I hope so," he said. And then he smiled, too.

Ms. Suza, who'd been hovering in the background, stepped up. "Mr. Peters, one thing you need to know." She sounded like she wished she didn't have to say this but she did. "I'm going to try to locate True's true owner."

"I understand. Till you do, I'll think of myself as foster care."

Gladys

First Mama tried the number on the LOST DOG flyer, but no one answered her message.

Next she tried Mrs. Marsh, who told her the name of the woman who owned the house where True had lived.

The woman turned out to be the mother of twins Mama had babysat years ago. She and Mama talked forever and a day about how the twins were doing now and how they still remembered how wonderful Ms. Suza was, and then she and Mama talked about how hard it was to get good tenants. Hearing about the abandoned dog, the woman gave Mama the motorcycle man's name and number.

Mama tried to call him. Two, three, four times she tried, leaving messages he never returned.

Gladys reported all this to Jude.

"Do you think she'll give up?" he asked.

"Never. She's incredibly stubborn about certain things."

"So that's where you get it."

"I'll take that for a compliment."

Jude

The first night Pookie stayed with Mr. Peters, she howled. *Howled.* If you thought her bark was bad? At last even Mom couldn't stand it. She told Jude to get his butt over there. When Pookie saw him, she went into such a tailspin she knocked him over. Knocking over somebody his size wasn't easy. Jude wound up sleeping on Mr. Peters's couch. That living room was so tidy, Jude was scared to even fart. (Pookie wasn't, though.) She started out lying on the floor, but it wasn't long till she was next to him, her snout in his armpit.

Who knew a dog could love an armpit?

When Auntie Jewel heard about Pookie, she showed up with a dog bed, a leather collar, an expandable leash, and enough toys to open a dog nursery school. Mr. Peters blushed as she thanked him for being so kind.

"This dog's a diamond in the rough," Auntie Jewel said with a wink. "If we took her to a groomer, she'd be a real beauty."

"Just like you to suggest a doggy beauty salon," Mom said.

"How 'bout you?" Auntie Jewel said. "I'll treat you to a makeover to celebrate your new job."

"Don't jinx me!" Jude's mother cried. "I didn't get it yet!"

But two days later, she did.

The same day Ms. Suza finally got the call from Pookie's owner.

Gladys

She'd just come home from school. The sprouts were having an afternoon snack, and for every Teddy Graham that went in their mouths, three hit the floor. Angela was cleaning up spilled juice and Mama was changing Mateo when her phone sang out.

"Get that for me, sugar?" Mama said.

Gladys picked it up. "Hello?"

"Yes ma'am. I'm returning a call from Suzanna?"

It was him. She knew it. Gladys's fingers tightened around the phone. Inside her, that dim, cold cave opened out again. This time it yawned so wide, her chest seemed to crack in two. Before she knew what was happening, words came pouring out.

"What is wrong with you?" she cried into the phone. "How could you do it? How could you just leave like that? What kind of human being are you?"

"Hang on! Who's this?"

"She waited for you! She looked for you! She didn't understand! Didn't you ever stop to think how—"

"Sugar." Mama was taking the phone from her. She touched Gladys's cheek. "Let me do this, okay?"

Gladys couldn't stand it. She grabbed Sophie, carried her outside, and sat on a swing. Sophie twisted around to look at her in wonder.

"Please don't talk," Gladys said. "Just let me hold you, okay?"

"Okay." Sophie rested her head on Gladys's chest.

A content, cozy sprout makes for a heavy load. While she waited for whatever would happen, Gladys's arms and legs went to sleep. Sophie wiped a dirty finger on her vintage silk vest. Yet Gladys held on to her, because otherwise she would fly into a million pieces.

A piece of bark broke loose from the reptile tree, falling to the earth with a small, brittle sigh. New, creamy bark peeked out, looking so tender and fragile Gladys could hardly bear it. With one foot she pushed the swing back and forth, back and forth.

Until at last the back door opened and she watched her mother cross the yard, watched her eye the other swing as if she'd like to sit there, if only she wasn't too large. Instead she dragged over a lawn chair and set it so she and Gladys were knee to knee.

Her face was serene, the face of someone who knew she'd made the right decision. With a small shock, Gladys realized that this was the first time in days Mama hadn't looked anxious. Her arms tightened around Sophie.

"He was calling from Montana," Mama said. "He says it's beautiful out there—big-sky country. A great place for a motorcycle. He—his name is George—George says he'll probably stay there, at least for now." Her brow flushed dark pink. "When I asked about True, he told me he'd gotten her at the pound when she was just a pup, about two years ago. George said he'd had dogs since he was a boy but never one like her. He said she was kookie—kookie Pookie. He sounded like he was really fond of her."

Gladys swallowed down the bad taste rising in the back of her mouth.

"He never meant to leave her, but things between him and his girlfriend got too hard, so he had to hit the road. He'd hoped Pookie would cheer her—her name is Iris—he hoped Pookie might comfort Iris after he was gone." Mama shook her head and sighed. "I don't think he meant any harm. He's just one sad, clueless man."

"No he's not!" The words burst from Gladys. "He's selfish and heartless. Mama! Don't let him off the hook! Admit it, he's bad! Say it!"

"When I told him Pookie had gotten loose and Iris moved without finding her, he was shocked. Sugar, the man actually couldn't speak for a moment. He said he'd track down Iris and tell her we'd found Pookie. He seemed to hope she'd still want the dog back."

Gladys hugged Sophie so tight, the little girl squealed in protest. Gladys's arms and legs, numb by now, prickled painfully awake. When Mama put a hand on her knee, Gladys looked at her bitten nails and knew: her mother had agreed with selfish, heartless George. She'd told him to call poor, wicked Iris. Mama, who had enough love and forgiveness inside her for everyone, even for George and Iris, Mama who always found the good in others, Mama who had hope enough for the whole wide world: Mama would believe it was the right thing to do.

"Don't keep the sad inside," Sophie whispered, patting Gladys's cheek.

"I told George that, even though he and I had only talked a short time, I could tell he never meant to hurt Pookie. I said, *You want the best for her, don't you?* and he said *Yes, ma'am,*

I do. I said, *You want her to have the most loving home possible, don't you?* And he said, *You got it, Miss Suza!*"

Tiny needles stabbed Gladys's arms and legs, her hands and feet. Something in Mama's face was changing.

"I said, George, we've already found that very home for her."

Gladys slid forward off the swing. Her legs folded up beneath her, and she and Sophie landed in a heap on the ground. Sophie shouted in glee.

"Do it again!" she demanded.

Mama hunkered down beside them and put her arms, arms big enough to circle the world, around them both.

"I told him Pookie had found the place she belongs, with people who will love her forever, no matter what."

"Thank you, Mama! Thank you thank you thank you!"

"You don't need to thank me. You're the one who found her that home. You found her the place she truly belongs."

Gladys rested her head on Mama's shoulder. Wordless communication flew between them.

Like you found me. Gladys.

And you found us. Mama.

Gladys could still feel the cave gaping inside her. Would it always be there? Maybe. She didn't know. But now its hollows were filled with warmth and golden light. Not filled. *Overflowing.*

"Let your happy out," Sophie said, wriggling in between them.

Jude

Every morning before school, he went next door to take Pookie for a walk. The world was quiet then. A different kind of quiet from the fortress, where it felt like you were hiding out, keeping the world away. This quiet was more like being *in* the world. Being part of it in a good way. Like you belonged. Pook would sniff the grass and he'd look at the trees, their leaves drifting down. Soon they'd be bare and you'd be able to see how their branches reached for the sky. He liked that.

Mom left real early because it was thirty miles to her new job. Plus the car sometimes stalled out and it took a while to get it going again. So Jude was in charge of dropping off Spider, who nowadays had a fit if you didn't call him Silas, though guess who was still going to call him Spider no matter how mad it made him? When they got to her house, Gladys was always ready. Now that it was chilly she wore a fur jacket with big sparkly buttons. Faux fur, she told him, like that was an important fact to know. Half a block from school they split up because school was still a messed-up place and Jude wasn't about to get punked. Gladys said she hoped he'd overcome that inhibition at some point.

That girl.

Mom still said no way under the sun she'd have a dog in her house.

But with her first paycheck, she bought ten pounds of fancy dog food and brought it over to Mr. Peters. And when Jude went to say good night to Pook, if he stayed longer than he was supposed to, sometimes long enough to watch some TV (it turned out Mr. Peters was a fan of WrestleMania) with Pookie's head on his knee, Mom didn't seem to notice.

Even though she noticed everything.

☀ Gladys

Spider-Silas was a real handful. Mama adored him.

Some afternoons, when Jude came to pick his little brother up, he'd be playing so nicely, Jude would hang around awhile. He'd eat a snack, even do his homework, Mateo drooling on his shoulder. One afternoon, they put Spider and Sophie in the double stroller and took them to the library, where Sophie forced them to watch her interminable puppet show and Spider knocked down some kid's block tower. They were buckling the sprouts into the stroller to start home when Gladys looked up to find Chickie and another girl coming toward her. They wore matching black puffy jackets and chartreuse scrunchies.

"Hey, Gladys."

"Hey, Chickie."

"This is my friend Morgan. She goes to St. Joe's."

"This is Jude. He goes to our school."

"I know," Chickie said.

Morgan fingered her ponytail and regarded Jude with interest. He, of course, remained perfectly oblivious.

"We just went to a baking class upstairs," Chickie said. "Want a cookie?"

"Me!" Spider and Sophie cried. "Me me!"

"No eating in the library," the librarian called, and then she winked.

Chickie wrapped some cookies in a napkin and gave them to Gladys.

"Okay," Chickie said. "Well. Bye."

As she and Morgan headed toward the door, Chickie glanced back. She wiggled her eyebrows at Gladys the way they used to, and without thinking, Gladys wiggled hers back.

She and Jude pushed the clumsy stroller into the elevator, went down a level, and pushed it outside. The sun was already low in the sky and Jude stopped to make sure both kids were zipped up. Gladys knew he wouldn't ask about Chickie, and that was a relief. Friendship was complicated. Everything was complicated if you thought about it for more than two minutes, which of course Gladys did, which she couldn't help doing, which she never, as long as she lived and breathed, planned to stop doing.

Infinite. The world held infinite things to ponder.

Even so, sometimes it was nice to let your brain drift a little. Not try to find words for things. The words would always be there, hovering just out of sight, hidden in the crooks of the tree lawn trees or the yellow glow of a streetlight. But sometimes it was restful not to reach for them. To just be. To take a bite of a truly delicious cookie. To listen to the low thump of the stroller on the bumpy sidewalk and to Spider and Sophie composing yet another repulsive poop song, to see the lamps switching on in the windows, to watch Jude puff out silvery clouds of breath, to lift your head and spy the first star through the spiky branches of a tree that you now knew was a ginkgo.

Jude

Ginkgo. Sycamore. Oak.

Almost home, where Pookie would be waiting for their walk. First he'd say goodbye, for now, to Gladys. Who was smiling to herself, for once not saying a word.

Maple. Oak. Sassafras.

Star.

She saw it, too, he could tell.

Make a wish, he thought.

But for the first time in his life, guess who couldn't think of anything to wish for?

Acknowledgments

So many people helped True find her way home!

Adoption is complex, and each child experiences it in his or her own way. The many conversations that Theresa Carroll and I have shared over the years taught me so much. Cassie Thomas's sensitive, perceptive reading was so helpful. Gladys and I owe them both thanks up to the moon and stars.

My brilliant early reader, Shelley Pearsall, saw the True heart of this book before I did and gave me the encouragement I needed to keep going.

As always, I'm grateful to my writing sisters, the Scorchettes and the Mean Girls of Tahoe, for their infinite support, wisdom, and wit. What would I do without our shared laughter?

Margaret Ferguson, editor for the ages, has been with this story every step of the way. Copy editor Chandra Wohleber's help was invaluable, as was Drew Seeger's. How lucky I am to have a room in Holiday House!

I can never thank my family enough for continuing to believe in me no matter what. And now that I am a nana, writing for children is, if possible, even more of a privilege and joy.

This is the last book I'll do with my beloved friend and agent, Sarah Davies, now retired. I'll never forget the day she called to offer me representation. She changed my life. Thank you, dear Sarah, for everything.